1: GO FOR IT, FEN!

"Don't worry, I'm going!" I yelled, and slammed the kitchen door, before going up-stairs two at a time, shutting and locking my bedroom door, and flinging myself down on my bed in floods of angry, hopeless tears.

The worst thing of all – the thing that stuck out like a skyscraper on a green hill – was what Mum said about the café. Well, I've told you I'm single-minded and I'm very determined and nothing was going to make me apologize to Mum. Nothing. Not even the knowledge that I might have to say goodbye to the café job…

Also in the Café Club series by Ann Bryant:

Leah Discovers Boys
Luce and the Weird Kid
Jaimini and the Web of Lies

1: GO FOR IT, FEN!

Ann Bryant

Hippo

Thanks to Viv Lowe for her invaluable help

Scholastic Children's Books,
Commonwealth House, 1–19 New Oxford Street,
London WC1A 1NU, UK
a division of Scholastic Ltd
London ~ New York ~ Toronto ~ Sydney ~ Auckland

First published by Scholastic Ltd, 1996

Copyright © Ann Bryant, 1996

ISBN 0 590 13424 8

Typeset by TW Typesetting, Midsomer Norton, Avon

Printed by Cox & Wyman Ltd, Reading, Berks.

All rights reserved

10 9 8 7 6 5 4 3 2 1

The right of Ann Bryant to be identified as the author
of this work has been asserted by her in accordance with the
Copyright, Designs and Patents Act, 1988.

For Jim, Jody and Carly

Chapter 1

Hi. My name's Fen and I'm thirteen years old. I live in a town called Cableden. All my friends live in Cableden and we all go to the same school. I've got shoulder-length brown hair and quite a freckly face. I'm rather thin, I like to do things quickly so I'm not particularly patient. I'm also a bit of a tomboy, always in jeans or leggings. But the main thing about me is that I'm very determined and single-minded. At the moment I'm feeling determined to crack the problem of trying to earn money.

If we take it that I have a minimum of three years schooling still stretching darkly before me, and if Mum and Dad get their way we can bump that up to five, this means that apart from occasional highlighted days, such as birthdays and Christmas, we are talking poverty for the next five years. Unless of course you count pocket money. And let's face it, pocket money isn't really worth counting.

I don't want to give the impression that I'm a horrible, mercenary person, but if you're anywhere round thirteen, I'm sure you'll agree it's tough when you're not supposed to babysit, and there's absolutely nothing else going.

Yes, OK, there are paper rounds, but believe me if you're a girl in our area you don't stand a chance. The boys have got it totally sewn up. If one day a boy gives up his paper round, the next day another one has taken over. Just like that! No one says a word, let alone advertises the fact that there is a job vacancy. It just happens – smooth as changing gear in an automatic car – no seams at all – just a new boy on the paper round, and we girls standing around wearing cross looks and shrugging our shoulders at the unfairness of it all.

So one day, the six of us in my group of really good friends got together. It was a wet break at school and we were sitting in the classroom. This is how our conversation went:

ME (the ambitious one): I know what I'm going to do. I'm going to see if I can get a job at *The Café*...

TASH (the peacemaker) *and my best friend. Dark hair in a sort of bob and dark twinkling eyes, really pretty, good all rounder, popular, kind, the most "normal" of us all, and the least selfish of us all*: You can't, Fen, you're under age.

ME (very single-minded, remember): My aunt Jan is the manageress there. She'll get me in.

JAIMINI (the brainy one) *and also really beautiful with big dark eyes, very long, black hair and that lovely coffee-coloured skin that comes from having a black father and a white mother. You pronounce her name Jay-m-nee by the way, but sometimes we shorten it to Jaimes, like the boy's name*: Do you think your mum'd let you, even if your aunt agreed? I mean, with homework and all that?

ME: Hm, that's a point...

ANDY (the daring one) *whose real name is Agnès. Her mum's French so that makes her half French. You pronounce Agnès, Ann-yes, which is much softer and nicer than the English pronunciation, but we've finished up by calling her Andy anyway, so it doesn't really apply. She's the smallest of us all, dark, with very short, cropped hair, and brown eyes. She's also really good at sport, and there's nothing she wouldn't dare to do*: Don't let that stop you, Fen. Go for it.

LUCE (the crazy one) *who's outgoing and outrageous in every way, including the way she dresses. She's got thick, quite short, palish auburn hair that gets tangled easily, freckles and green eyes. She's a great practical joker, always opening her mouth and putting her foot in it, if you see what I mean! Oh, and Luce is short for Lucy*: Yeah, go for it Fen, and if your mum isn't happy, tell her we'll all help.

ME (can be sarcastic): That will delight her, of course.

LEAH (the musician) *with absolutely no idea how talented she is. She plays the violin and the piano, she's very sensitive and self-critical. She's pretty with a calm, still face, and very long, pale hair usually scraped back into a bun or something. She's also the biggest worrier of us all*: Luce's idea may not be so crazy. There are six days of the week and six of us. Your mum probably wouldn't let you work every day, Fen, but if we all took turns, then nobody's school work would suffer.

LUCE: Brilliant, Leah! You've cracked it. We all work in the café one day each after school, and one lucky person gets to do Saturday, then we swap the rota for the next week so we all get to do a Saturday.

TASH (like I said, the least selfish): But, Fen, it's up to you. It was your idea in the first place, so if you can get the job without us, we won't mind.

ME: That's OK, Tash. I think Leah's really hit on something good.

ANDY: What's so great about Saturdays?

LUCE (grinning wickedly): No school, more time, more money!

ME: What if Aunt Jan says we're too young?

JAIMINI: Our age is definitely against us.

LEAH: Why not cross that bridge when we come to it?

LUCE: I say we go for it. I've always wanted to work in a café. In fact, as soon as I get home I'm going to practise balancing plates all the way up my arm. Just think, this will be my passport to the adult world. I can already think of four ways of adapting that plain-looking black and white uniform you have to wear in the caff.

ANDY: You're mad, Luce. I see it as good training, all that walking about, dodging between tables, carrying heavy trays. I can train *and* earn money at the same time.

TASH: I could certainly do with the money. I'm nowhere near my target for that soda stream for Mum's birthday present.

JAIMINI: The money'd be great but…

ME: But what?

JAIMINI: I just can't imagine my parents agreeing to my working in a café during term time, or during any time, come to that.

LUCE: Don't worry, Jaimes, we'll get the parents who think it's a good idea to work on the ones who aren't so keen.

Everybody agreed with that, and we talked till the end of break about the best way to approach our mothers, and most importantly of all, the best way for me to approach my aunt Jan.

It was double science after break, not the best lesson for trying to have a discreet conversation with your friend, because of old Hawkenbury, the ancient science teacher who was always peering at you through the rows of Bunsen burners or over the top of the test-tube racks.

"Fenella Brooks, too much gas coming from your mouth and not enough from your experiment," he barked at me. Then he rocked with laughter while looking round at the rest of the class to check they all appreciated his little joke. I took the opportunity to have another whisper to Tash.

"I'm going to keep a little portable tape recorder hidden somewhere in the café, then if I observe something really interesting I can get it straight on tape while it's fresh in my mind."

"What, for your book?" Tash asked, instantly understanding my enthusiasm as any best friend would.

I grinned at her and nodded, then we studied the blue stuff in our test-tubes as though our lives depended on it, because Hawkenbury was on the war path again.

"I hope that isn't Fenella and Natasha talking again?" he observed.

"Oh no, sir," we assured him, glancing up then assuming our intense gazing act.

Tash knows it's one of my ambitions to write a novel some day. I've almost persuaded her to try one too. I reckon this café venture might inspire us both.

After double science it was lunch, then we just had French and maths to get through, before we could go home and set wheels in motion. The plan was that if I got the OK from Aunt Jan, I would phone Tash who would immediately phone Andy, and so on, so we'd all know at the first opportunity, then we could spend the rest of the evening working on our parents. The next day we would meet and tell each other how we got on.

We were all so excited that the afternoon lessons were a complete waste of time. I don't know about the others, but apart from learning that the French for head-lice is *les poux*, (pronounced pooh!), I didn't take in a single thing all afternoon.

As soon as the end-of-school bell went, I grabbed my bag, did a big fingers crossed sign at Tash across the classroom – the other four were in different workgroups for most lessons – and scrambled out of the classroom, banging my hips twice on sticking-out desks. The corridors, as usual, were so crowded it was impossible to make a quick getaway. I followed the general flow of black skirts and trousers and swinging school bags, doing a few neat overtaking moves whenever the chance came up, then finally I was out of the main doors.

"Good luck, Fen." That was Andy emerging from year-eight's door.

"Same to you. See you."

It took exactly seven minutes to half walk, half run into the town centre. The café was between a jeweller's and an optician's. Big welcoming windows were set in bright green framework. Through them the bustling happy atmosphere of the café shone into the street. Everyone who passed couldn't help looking in. Most people slowed right down when they were passing because the café was like a magnet, and some were actually drawn to going in.

Inside, at the tables, there were mothers with toddlers and groups of families and friends. Some leaned forwards and chatted nineteen to the dozen, some leaned back and gazed out of the window. I noticed that one old lady at a corner table was gazing at me. She had a rather square face, glasses and a headscarf. She was clutching her handbag on the table in front of her. My imagination took over, as it often does, because people fascinate me. This was no ordinary old lady, I told myself. This was a fugitive, someone on the run from the police, merely disguised as an old lady. And what was in the handbag?

I came to my senses then because another old lady joined the first one at her table. This second one had obviously just been to the loo or something. The first lady leaned forward confidentially to her friend, and whispered something with a jerk of the head in my direction.

It occurred to me that I must have seemed terribly rude staring in through the window. My dad is always saying, "For goodness sake, Fen, stop gawping." Poor Dad. He lives in a family of stare bears. There's me, my sister Rachel (aged nine), and my sister Emmy (aged five). When we all stare, Dad gets in a real state about it. "Stop staring, Dee," he hisses at Mum, and she will break out of her trance and say, "Was I staring? Oh sorry, I didn't realize."

Anyway, back to the present. I pushed open the café door, glanced round, raised a hand in a tiny wave to Becky, one of the waitresses, then after a nice, reassuringly sane smile at the old ladies, I made for the kitchen at the back, where I guessed my aunt Jan would be.

"Hi, Jan," I said, feeling a sudden gush of nervousness as I remembered the importance of this meeting.

"Watcha, Nelly!"

I rolled my eyes at Kevin the chef, whose favourite pastime was trying to make people mad. He was actually such a nice person it was impossible to be mad at him.

"If you weren't so good at your job, I'd sack you for being nasty to one of my favourite nieces," Jan said, with a wink at Kevin. It was true he was a brilliant chef, and I'd often heard Jan telling Mum how hard he worked, and how she could never be satisfied with any other chef, because Kevin's act was too tough to follow.

"My name is *Fen*, OK!" I told his back firmly. He wasn't listening. He was back to work, clearing up his pans and bowls and basins after the busy lunch period.

Jan and I exchanged a smile. I never call her aunt or aunty. She doesn't like it. She once said that "Aunt Jan" made her sound at least ninety-four degrees in the shade, whereas "Jan" sounded more like thirty-two, so naturally she preferred the latter. She's actually forty-one but she's very fit and slim from running the café, and also from running around *in* the café. It makes her seem younger that she's young in spirit, even though she's also quite strict and very wise and thoughtful.

"How are you doing, pet? Haven't seen you for ages."

"I'm OK … but … Jan…" I began hesitantly. I couldn't continue because Louise came rushing in and squealed, "No, Kevin, don't!"

"Sorry. Too late," Kevin answered calmly as he dipped a fatty frying pan into the lovely hot sudsy water that Louise had got all ready to wash glasses and cutlery.

"Oh, Kevin!" Louise groaned. "How can

someone so good-looking be such an utter pain?" she went on.

Kevin just smiled. It was true. He was good-looking – small, dark and wiry with curly black hair – about twenty-one I'd guess.

"Two seconds, pet…" Jan said to me and dived back into the café. Almost immediately she popped her head back round the kitchen door and said, "Jug of water for table seven, Louise."

"Coming up," answered Louise, drying her hands. "'Scuse me."

This was to me. It made me feel silly standing there like a statue while everybody else was so busy. Jan came hurtling back in through the swing doors. I opened my mouth to speak.

"Two seconds, pet," and she snatched a tray and whizzed out again. I could hear her talking to customers, then I heard the till clicking and buzzing. When she reappeared, she grabbed my hand, said, "We'll get two minutes peace out here," and led me into the yard at the back, where we both sat down at a little garden table with benches attached.

"So what brings you to the madhouse?" she asked, cupping her chin in her hands and levelling her eyes at me.

"Well … I was wondering…"

This was it.

"That sounds ominous," Jan remarked. "Let me guess. Money? Um, advice? No, silly me, you'd go to your mum for advice, she's always been much the more sensible of the two of us…"

"It's sort of both," I ventured, "and a favour as well."

"Mmm," she murmured, non-committally, "go on then."

"Well, you see, I was wondering whether … you needed any help in your café?"

"I see where this is leading, pet, and I'm sorry, I won't waste your time by raising your hopes. I'm afraid I couldn't afford to take on anyone else, much as I'd like to. I've got Debra first thing in the morning, then Mark or Becky joins her, then Louise takes over with either Mark or Becky, from three till six … I'm really sorry, Fen."

"Oh."

That was all I could think of to say. My body didn't seem to belong to me any more. It felt tired and heavy and kind of stuck to that table. For some reason not one of the six of us had considered the possibility that Jan wouldn't actually want anybody. We'd all gaily assumed that the job would just be there waiting for us to jump into.

Jan put her hand over mine.

"Sorry, Fen, you look so disappointed."

The back door opened and Louise stumbled out as though escaping from a fire or something.

"God, it's hot in there," she said, leaning back against the cold stone wall. "There must be easier ways of earning a living than working in an amazingly popular café."

Jan smiled. "Come on, better get back to it."

"Oh, the pressure, the pressure!" Louise murmured dramatically as she entered the fray again.

"I'll see you tomorrow night, pet. I'm popping round to give your mum that recipe.

Hey … what about babysitting to earn some money?"

"Not allowed till you're fourteen."

"Paper round?"

"Boys have got them all."

"I'll think about it. See you tomorrow."

And with that she was gone.

I walked round the café instead of going back through it, and carried on home slowly and despondently.

"Whatever's the matter?" was my mum's greeting, catching sight of my miserable face.

"Nothing," I answered, because I couldn't be bothered to explain.

"Well, it must be a very serious case of nothing," Mum answered, trying but failing to get a smile out of me. "Or would you rather I minded my own business?"

"No, it's not that. It's just…" I hesitated because I had carefully prepared a speech all about the café, to ask Mum's permission, but of course now it didn't really matter any more. I could say any old thing.

"Well, you see, we had it all worked out, me and the others. We were going to do one evening each after school, so we wouldn't miss homework or anything."

"Do what? Where?"

"Work in Jan's café, to get a bit of money … but it's no good, cos she doesn't need anyone. She's got Louise…"

"That's a shame because it sounds, on the face of it, like an excellent idea. You'd have to get work permits from the LEA of course, but that wouldn't be a problem. And Jan would be the perfect employer. I mean, nobody else would dare to take on six different girls in any one week, but Jan at least knows you all. Also, I can't imagine anyone else needing extra help from say four o'clock till six, whereas the café's quite busy then… What a shame she doesn't need anyone."

I looked at Mum and thought how surprising life could be. I mean, I'd just calmly said a few words about the café, and here was Mum, equally calmly agreeing that it was an excellent idea, even talking about work permits, with absolutely no sign of any "well-I-don't-know-I'll-have-to-speak-to-your-father" type speeches. And yet Jan – lovely, accommodating, wise, helpful Jan – didn't want me... "Sorry, pet, try a paper round." Life was weird.

"Jan's coming round tomorrow night."

"Yeah. She told me."

"I'll have a word with her."

"What good will that do?"

"Probably none. We'll see."

That was Mum's favourite expression – "We'll see". It covered everything in the world that wasn't definite.

"Can I phone Tash?"

"Yes, go on."

So I got ready to depress my friends by setting the chain of phone calls going.

Chapter 2

Another wet break. The weather matched our feelings. Everyone had been so fed up when they'd heard my bad news the previous evening, yet today they were going out of their way to say nice things, which shows I've got really good friends.

"Well, my parents wouldn't have let me work in the café even if your aunt Jan had said it was OK, so there would only have been five of you," Jaimini said, quietly.

"And I would have messed up the rota because I'd never be able to do a Thursday," Leah added.

"Yes, of course, your violin lesson," said

Tash, thoughtfully. "Come to think of it, Fen, we've all got clubs or practices or something at least one day after school. It would have been quite complicated to organize."

"Yes, what about my netball practice and running club?" Andy asked.

I didn't say anything. She wasn't looking for an answer. They were all just scraping the barrel for reasons why it wouldn't have worked, in order to cheer me up. Luce's next words proved it.

"Well, I did a couple of sketches of how I could adapt that black and white gear, and they looked awful. Then I tried balancing plates on my arm. I've broken four so far. Mum wasn't at her happiest last night, I can tell you."

I laughed along with the others but I didn't feel any better. We just seemed so close to having a brilliant project in our lives. I mean, it must have been brilliant if even Mum thought so.

"Is your name Fenella Brooks?"

I glanced up to see a boy of about fifteen

with a very modern haircut. He didn't seem ill at ease in our classroom. My first thought was, Help! What have I done wrong? Is this going to be a message from a teacher saying I've got to stay for detention after school because I was seen running in the corridors or something?

"Yes, I'm Fen," I said, probably sounding worried.

"So you're Jan Geeson's niece?"

I had to think about that one for a second. Jan who? Oh, of course, Aunt Jan...

"Yes, why?"

"My sister Louise works at your aunt's café."

"Louise is your sister. Right. I saw her yesterday, but only for a second. She came outside for a breather when I was talking to Jan."

"Yeah, well the thing is..."

The boy suddenly seemed less sure of himself. Tash and the others were all ears. Come to think of it, the whole class was all ears. That was because it's very unusual for a

year-ten boy to saunter into year-eight girls'
territory and strike up a conversation.

"The thing is, Louise heard what you and
your aunt were saying, and she asked me to
get you to go into the café again … to have a
word with her."

"Oh," was all I could manage.

"Something to do with the job?" asked
Andy, who probably thought I was behaving
amazingly dumbly.

The boy turned to Andy. "Could be," he
told her, simply. "Louise wants to work in a
hairdresser's, but it's a problem at the
moment, so she's filling in at the café."

I opened my mouth to speak, but he was
gone.

"Don't forget to call in," he called back to
me as he disappeared through the classroom
door into the corridor.

"Well, if Louise wants to do hairdressing,
maybe things will turn out all right in the
end," Luce said loudly, over the harsh sound
of the end-of-break bell.

I went to get my books sorted out for the

next lesson. An inkling of hope had re-appeared, but I still felt impatient. I wanted that job right now, not "in the end".

After school, I did exactly as I had done the day before – battled my way down endless corridors, then out of the main doors into the pouring rain. At least I'd got my coat. I know it's not very cool to wear a coat, but all the kids who hadn't got coats were soaked to the skin which didn't look all that cool, I can tell you.

By the time I got to the café my hair looked as though I'd just washed it. I collapsed through the door into that lovely cosy atmos-phere, where I proceeded to drip my way through to the kitchen. I tried not to touch any chairs, I didn't want to send little streams of water from my soaking coat down some poor unsuspecting customer's back. I giggled at the thought of this, and one or two people looked up from their crumpets and tea to give me an odd look.

Jan was at the other side of the café with her back to me, so I crossed straight through to the kitchen where I found Kevin at the back door, signing for a delivery of wine, and Louise buttering scones as though her life depended on it. She glanced up.

"Hi, Fen – two seconds…"

I was beginning to get used to this phrase. It must be café-speak. She rushed out and rushed back in again, then flopping down in a chair in the corner she repeated her phrase from the previous day, "Oh, the pressure, the pressure."

"Is it really that bad?" I asked.

"Certainly is." She lowered her voice. "Especially when you don't really want to be here."

"Your brother said you want to work in a hairdresser's…"

"Yeah, I do, only I don't drive, and the problem is that there are only two hairdresser's in Cableden, one much nicer than the other, but anyway neither of them has any vacancies."

I was beginning to wonder why she'd asked her brother to get me to go and see her. She explained with her next words. "I asked Michael to get you to pop in because I felt a bit sorry for you yesterday. I couldn't help hearing what you and Jan were saying, and I just wanted you to know that I won't be here for ever. As soon as something comes up at ClairHair – that's the really good local salon – I'll be off like a shot."

"Oh, right," I said. "Well, thanks for telling me. Do they come up very often – jobs in hairdressers'?"

The moment I'd asked it, I felt really juvenile, but it was the impatient side of my nature coming to the fore again.

"Lyn's been there for at least a year, I reckon."

That did it. My spirits, which had been on a yo-yo string for the last twenty-four hours, plummeted to the ground as I mentally wrote off the café job for another year.

"Let's cross our fingers," said Louise, as she set back to work.

"Hello, pet," said a familiar voice as Jan pushed her way into the kitchen with her usual speed. "Can't keep away, eh? My goodness, you're soaked to the skin. Here you go, have a hot cup of tea."

Before I could say a word, she'd thrust a white cup and saucer into my hands and the steam from the tea began to warm my face. Then she offered me a toasted crumpet and I began to feel very cosy, sitting there drying off and warming up. Mark was on duty with Louise. He called out an order to Kevin, stuffed the top copy from his pad on to a pinboard and disappeared. Kevin was sweating, I noticed, as he dumped the last case of wine in a corner, and bent down to peer into the bottom oven.

I looked round the kitchen. There was the old-fashioned Aga, spice racks, deep bright bowls of fruit, dried flowers hanging from dark beams and heaped up in curvy, wicker baskets and a tall, old pine cupboard. Then amongst this stood the dishwasher, two enormous freezers, three microwaves, the fridge, the grill, the milk machine, the washing machine and two cookers, all bright and white and modern. There were tea towels hanging up to dry over the Aga, lovely old skillets hanging high on hooks and shiny new pans sitting on shelves with teapots and trays.

The noise of chatter and laughter seeped under the doorway, except when the door was opened, and then it burst into the kitchen briefly and loudly and I caught a glimpse of teatime customers. It was like watching a television programme. It would have been so brilliant to work here – so much material for my first novel. I sighed and finished my tea.

"Bye then, Jan. Thanks for the tea."

"Bye, pet. Take care."

It was still raining so I half walked and half ran home. As soon as I walked in Emmy, my five-year-old-sister, rushed up and said, "Tash phoned. You've got to phone her back right now." And she thrust the phone into my hands. Rachel, my nine-year-old sister appeared behind her and said, "Emmy, it wasn't *that* urgent. She just said phone when-ever, Fen."

"She said very urgent," insisted Emmy.

Rachel gave me a look that said, "Little sisters, who needs them?" behind Emmy's back.

I said I'd phone in a couple of minutes which I hoped was a good enough compromise to keep them both happy. Occasionally it can be hard work having two younger sisters, but most of the time we all get on well together because there's a big enough age gap between us to stop any rivalry.

I've got a bedroom of my own. It's very small but at least it's my own. Emmy and Rachel share a room that's bigger than mine. If ever I'm sleeping over at a friend's house, I let Rachel have my room for the night. Mum says it makes her laugh because although Rachel and Emmy are always desperate to sleep separately, as soon as they have the chance to escape each other for a night, out come their walkie-talkies and they talk for ages instead of going to sleep.

I tapped in Tash's number. After one ring she answered.

"Fen?"

"Yes, how did you know?"

She didn't bother to answer that.

"Listen Fen, I was thinking about what Louise's brother said, about Louise wanting to work in a hairdresser's, and you know Mum's friend Elaine, well, she's got a salon at Brenendon. So I phoned her up on a hunch, and guess what, she's desperately looking for a good stylist. Her stylist left quite suddenly, so the advert for a new one hasn't even gone in the paper yet, but apparently it's in the *Cableden and District News* which comes out tomorrow, and loads of people are certain to apply for the job immediately. That's why I told Emmy to tell you to phone back the second you walked through the door. You've got to get hold of Louise as fast as poss, and tell her to phone Elaine and apply for it. I've got the number here. It's…"

"Tash, Tash, stop a second… Look, the bad news is that Louise doesn't drive. She told me just now that she could only possibly work in the salon at Cableden."

There was a silence that seemed to go on for ever.

"Sorry, Tash," I said softly, knowing that poor Tash would be feeling the same yo-yo emotions that I had felt earlier.

"So, that's that then," came Tash's despondent voice.

"Seems like it," I agreed.

We talked for a couple of minutes about a television programme we both wanted to watch, then we checked we were both going to write no more than two sides for science homework, and we were just about to ring off when I remembered something Tash had said.

"Did you speak to Emmy or Rachel earlier on?" I asked her.

"Both," she answered. "I wanted to be double sure you got the message, so when I'd told Emmy to get you to ring back the moment you walked in, I asked to speak to Rachel and I repeated the message to her."

"Oh, right."

"Why, Fen? Is there something wrong?"

"No, it's OK. I'll see you tomorrow. Bye."

"Bye."

I sat staring out of my bedroom window for

about five minutes thinking about what Tash had said, and wondering why the café had twice come within our grasp, only to be taken away again. Life didn't usually work like that and I wasn't about to give up. Then I thought about Rachel. Why had she deliberately told me there was no hurry to phone Tash back, when Tash had stressed to both Emmy and Rachel that it was really urgent? I decided to think about that later. The café problem was more important.

At the end of five minutes I thought I had the solution but time was against me. I had to move quickly, and first I had to get hold of Tash again. I tapped in her number and her sister Peta answered. That sounds like a boy's name I know, but it is a girl's name when it's spelt P-E-T-A. I didn't like the name at first, but now I like it so much that if ever I have a daughter, I'm thinking of calling her Peta.

Back to the phone call. My heart sank when I heard Peta's voice, because she's only just three and though she can be very entertaining, now was not the right moment for it.

"Who is it?" she piped up before I said a word.

"Hi, Peta, it's Fen here. Can I speak to Tash, please?"

"Hello, Fen."

Pause.

"Hello, Fenny Penny."

"Yes, I've said 'Hi' Peta, now could you be a very quick girl and get me Tash?"

"Yes."

"Go on, then."

"Fen?"

"Yes."

"Do you like sausages?"

"Yes, I love them. Could you get Tash, Peta?"

"I'm having sausages for tea."

"Well, that's great but…"

"Mum says my tummy'll pop if I eat more than three, but it's never popped before so I told her I'm having four today."

"Well, when I see you next time, you'll have to tell me how many you managed, but now could you be a good girl and quickly get me Tash?"

"OK."

Pause.

"Peta, are you still there?"

"Yes."

"Well, put the phone down and go and get Tash."

"OK."

And she rang off.

At that moment I could have killed her. I tapped in Tash's number again and after a couple of rings Tash answered.

"Tash. It's Fen. Peta was supposed to get you, but she put the phone down."

"I'll kill her."

Good, I thought, that'll save me a job.

"Listen, Tash, I've got a plan but we've got to act fast. Can you meet me at the café in ten minutes, and bring Elaine's number with you?"

"OK."

She put the phone down. Good old Tash. She's so quick to pick things up. It doesn't matter if it's school work or just what people are thinking or feeling. Perceptive – that's the word.

I called out hello and bye-bye to Mum. She asked where I was going and when I would be back. I told her the café and about an hour. She said I mustn't be late, I said I wouldn't, and then I was out of the door.

Ten minutes later Tash and I were in the kitchen at the café talking to Louise in hushed tones so Jan couldn't hear.

"The thing is, Louise, if you could persuade someone at ClairHair to go for the job at Elaine's, then you could work at ClairHair."

Louise looked doubtful and frowned.

"I'll think about it," she said, finally.

"But there isn't time to think," I persisted. "The advert'll be in the paper tomorrow morning. The job'll be gone by lunchtime."

Louise knitted her brows together.

"What are you suggesting, that I march into ClairHair and start telling people to try for a job at Elaine's so I can step neatly into their shoes? Nice idea girls, but out of the question, don't you think?"

It was Tash's and my turn to look thoughtful. Louise had firmly put us in our place and was now sprinkling cheese on to toast with her back to us. Tash and I looked at each other.

"Just tell me one thing," I asked Louise. "If there *was* a job at ClairHair, would you definitely want it if you had to start immediately?"

"If Jan would let me leave straight away, which I doubt," was Louise's rather depressing answer.

"See you soon then," I called, dragging Tash out through the back door.

"Come on, we're going to ClairHair," I told her. "We've got five minutes till it closes."

At exactly twenty-nine minutes past five we burst in through ClairHair's doors to find three surprised-looking hairdressers in lovely trendy uniforms consisting of a dark pink shirt, and black leggings and waistcoat, all sweeping the floor, wiping round basins, gathering curlers and clips, and generally clearing up at top speed.

They broke off for a second when we made our dramatic entry, but went straight back to work. We obviously weren't interesting enough to warrant any more attention. One of them smiled at us, though, so I decided to approach this one.

"'Scuse me," I said, "sorry to disturb you…" I suddenly felt really stupid. I wished at that moment that I could play the last two minutes in reverse and finish up outside the salon, but I couldn't and I had to say something. I looked at Tash for help. She bit her lip and looked down, which was a great help.

"Could I have a word with you?" I asked.

The girl, well, young woman – I guess she was about twenty-five – put her broom down against the wall and said, "Yeah, sure, come and sit down." Here was a smiling, helpful person, ready to listen to a silly thirteen-year-old. I liked her instantly.

"It's quite complicated," I went on.

"That's OK. Fire away," she said, which encouraged me to continue.

"There's a girl we know who works at the café in the High Street. She really wants to do hairdressing but she doesn't drive. Well, you know there are hardly any buses round here and they're all at the wrong times, well…"

I paused. The next bit was the tricky part.

"So you want to know if there are any vacancies here," said the woman, whose name was Lyn I noticed from her badge.

"Well, Louise has already found out there aren't any but…"

"That's where you're wrong," interrupted Lyn, "because as from next week I've got a new job at Rawsthorne, which means there will be a vacancy here. The only trouble is I think the lady in charge here has already got someone in mind for my job."

"Yes, she has," put in one of the hairdressers who was sweeping the floor. I didn't even look at her but I remember thinking I didn't like her tone of voice.

Tash and I rolled our eyes at each other as if to say "Not again". Just as soon as we got any really hopeful news our hopes were crushed again. The whole thing was getting unbelievable.

"Glenda," Lyn called out to a lady who had appeared from a back room. The lady's hair looked as though it was kept in its big cloudy halo shape by superglue and starch. Glenda clicked over to us on a pair of the highest heels I've ever seen. She must have been very small because Tash and I stood up straight as though in the presence of the Queen, and Glenda was only the same height as us, heels and all. Her badge also said MANAGERESS.

"These girls were wondering about the vacancy," Lyn began.

"Too young my dears, try again in a few years' time."

"No, it's not for us," Tash quickly assured her.

"For Louise," I blurted out.

"Louise Shrimpton?"

"Er, I'm not sure what her last name is."

"Works at the café?"

"Yes."

"I was just about to call her there, actually. She's been wanting a job here for ages. I told her she could have one as soon as one came up."

Again Tash and I exchanged looks. This time in slow motion as it dawned on us both that Louise would be leaving and *we* would be starting! Our eyes grew wide with happiness and we burst into war whoops and began dancing round clutching each other. Lyn and Glenda stared at us in amazement for about two seconds, then laughed with us even though they must have thought us totally bonkers. After a moment or two we all calmed down and Tash and I explained to them why we were so happy.

"God moves in mysterious ways," Glenda summed up, with a wink. When she winked there was a delay of a couple of seconds before her false eyelashes batted up and down. She may have looked weird but I really liked Glenda with her glossy pink lips and her stiff hair. She was warm and friendly. I suppose it's human nature to like someone who gives you good news, but I think I liked her anyway.

Tash and I walked home happily. We planned that I should talk to Mum and see how she suggested I tackle Jan, then once again I would set the chain going to Tash and the others so they could all work on their parents.

I didn't allow myself to feel totally happy. There was still a long way to go, but things were definitely looking up.

Chapter 3

I burst into the house.

"Mum! Where's Mum, Rachel?"

"Dunno, I think she went out."

"Went out? Well, who's looking after you and Emmy?"

"I'm looking after Emmy and no one's looking after me because you weren't here."

"Mum knew I was going out. She wouldn't just go out herself and leave you two alone."

Emmy muttered, "Nasty thing," which I think was aimed at me. Rachel took her hand, shrugged and went upstairs. I ran through the back door into the garden where I immediately saw Mum collecting chives.

"Hi. Rachel thought you'd gone out."

Mum frowned, looking puzzled, then carried on collecting chives and said, "Well, she was mistaken… Good day?"

"Yeah, guess what, it looks as though the café job is on after all!"

"Uh-huh."

Hang on a sec. Why was Mum just strolling back into the house with a handful of chives? She should have jumped up and hugged me and my good news. Where had all her enthusiasm gone?

"I thought you'd be pleased," I said, trailing after her.

"Has Jan changed her mind, then?"

"Mum, it wasn't her mind that needed changing. It was the situation. She didn't have a vacancy before but now she has."

"Really?"

"Yes. Louise, the girl who does the teatime shift at the moment, has got a job at a hairdresser's, and she's leaving as soon as she can."

I suddenly remembered something very important.

"Jan's coming round tonight, isn't she?"

"Yes she is, but don't get too excited, Fen, because when I spoke to her on the phone today, she said she was relieved, in a way, that she couldn't take you on, because six girls would be a bit much to keep track of. Although she knows you all, she doesn't know how good you are at working in a café, and it would be a difficult and embarrassing situation for her if one or two of you weren't up to scratch."

I tightened my lips and heaved a big sigh, thinking why do adults have to always look for the down side of things?

"I can see Jan's point of view, Fen. Say she had to get rid of two of you. There'd be only four left and how could you possibly organize a workable rota with all your commitments? Jan would never know if she was coming or going. She'd spend the entire time worrying that no one was going to turn up."

There was a knock at the door.

"Talk of the devil… It's open, Jan, come in."

Jan mimicked Mum's voice. "'She'd spend

the entire time worrying that no one was going to turn up.' Who would? Me?"

Mum laughed as her sister walked in.

"Eavesdropping again, Jan?" she asked.

"Sorry to interrupt your very interesting conversation that I couldn't help hearing."

"Would you like some tea or coffee or anything?" I asked her, which I thought was a smart move. "Let me show you how well I can make it."

"Uh-oh, I'm not sure I like the sound of this. I'll have some decaffeinated coffee, pet. So you've heard the news already have you, that Louise is leaving?"

"Yes, and Mum was just telling me what you're worrying about, but please, please, *please* give us a chance. We're all good workers. We'll all do our very best. I mean, at least with six of us, if one isn't working hard enough or something, that's only one bad day per week, but if you replaced Louise with only one person who turned out to be useless, that would be a disaster every day of the week, wouldn't it?"

Out of the corner of my eye I saw Mum smile.

"That was a long speech all in one breath," Jan commented, then in walked Rachel and Emmy.

"Aunty Jan!" cried Emmy, rushing over to Jan and climbing on to her lap.

"Hello, my cherry pie," said Jan, hugging Emmy.

I don't know if it was because she'd worked in a café for so long, but Jan always called her favourite children by food names, though never the same name twice. Cherry Pie was a new one.

At that point Rachel left the kitchen.

"Rachel, you haven't even said hello to Aunty Jan," Mum called after her, but there was no reply. So Mum got up, looking none too pleased, and went off to find Rachel.

Emmy scrambled down from Jan's knee, saying, "I'll get my sewing to show you."

That left Jan and me on our own.

"Pleeeeeeeease," I begged Jan.

· "Oh, the pressure, the pressure!" (More

café-speak you notice.)

"*Pleeeeeeeeeeeease.*" I was on my knees with praying hands.

"Look, I don't even know if you and your friends could cope properly. None of you has any experience, and I don't want customers being put off at the sight of thirteen-year-olds."

"Why don't you interview us? Then you'd see how sensible and mature we are."

"One thing at a time. Find out if you're all allowed to do the job first, then come back to me."

"*Yessss!*" I cried, triumphantly punching the air. "I'll get on the phone right away. And we'll all come to see you tomorrow after school."

"I'm making no promises mind…"

I didn't answer that. I just tore out of the room, grabbed the phone from the hall and leapt up to my bedroom, passing a grim-faced Mum on the way marching a blotchy-faced Rachel back to the kitchen. Whatever was the matter with Rachel? I'd find out later.

"Tash?" I said, about ten seconds later as her phone was picked up.

No answer.

Oh, no! Please God, spare me, not Peta again.

God obviously didn't hear me because Peta's voice piped up, "Who is it?"

"It's Fen."

"Not again."

(How funny we should both be thinking exactly the same thought.)

"'Fraid so."

The next thing that happened was that my ears were blasted off by the sound of Peta's extremely raised voice yelling out, "Tasha Basha, it's Fenny Penny."

This was followed by a peal of giggles, then, amazingly, Tash was on the phone.

"Hi, it's me. Guess what? We're through the first round."

"Hey, great!"

"Don't get too excited. Jan's going to need a bit of convincing about the six of us being OK. But at least she's got as far as telling us to find out if our parents are in agreement."

"Good, we're getting somewhere. I'll phone Leah straight away."

"No, phone Jaimini first. She'll need the most time to work on her parents."

"Good point. OK, see you tomorrow."

"Yeah, we'll plan our attack in morning break. Tell the others to make sure they're wearing the neatest possible version of the school uniform."

"Yeah, bye."

After Jan had gone I did my homework, then tapped on Rachel's door. Two voices answered. Emmy's said, "Come in," Rachel's said, "Go away." Then Emmy said, "Yeah, go away."

If I hadn't been so pleased about the café, I would have been quite upset because I didn't know why my sisters were suddenly waging war on me. All the same I didn't need any more problems so I decided to take Rachel's advice.

"Night-night, you two," I called through the door, then I went down to see Mum.

Dad had arrived back from work.

"Hi, you're late today, Dad."

"Blasted trains…" He grinned though and gave the top of my head a kiss. "What's all this café business your mum's been telling me about?"

Dad has two conversation modes: One – sensible. Two – flippant. If you want to have a sensible conversation and he's in his flippant mode, it can be very frustrating because he twists everything you're saying into a joke, and never comes up with any answers or agreements or disagreements or anything. But it *can* be very helpful… For example, if Mum has just told you off and Dad walks in, in his flippant mode, the telling off gets diluted by his witty remarks and in the end Mum is so busy laughing, she can't tell you off any more.

The other mode, the sensible one, is what I wanted him to be in at this moment, because I needed his agreement and his approval, so that I could go safely ahead into the next round, the "Aunt Jan round".

I looked at him. He certainly looked sensible, but it was difficult to tell from that opening question about the café. I took a deep breath and answered him in my most serious voice.

"Well, me, Tash, Jaimini, Leah, Luce and Andy – that's six of us – want to work one day each at Jan's café just for a couple of hours in the afternoon…"

"'Scuse me," Dad interrupted.

I stopped and waited.

"That's seven, not six."

I counted them slowly on my fingers for him. "Me, Tash, Jaimini, Leah, Luce and Andy. Six."

"Oh, sorry, it's just that last time you said, '*Well*, me, Tash, Leah, Jaimini, Andy and Luce,' and I assumed Well was a new friend – short for Wellemina or Wellarella or something."

"Oh, Dad, don't be stupid, *please*. This is very important." I looked at Mum for help and she gave the smallest of shakes of the head at Dad. He coughed and made a big thing of arranging his face into a frowning, serious look. I was beginning to get exasperated.

"I'm not talking about it if you're going to act like that, Dad."

"Look, I'm serious," he said, showing me his palms up, as if that proved anything. "Go on, tell me more."

"Well, there's nothing more to tell really. I just want to know if you think it's a good idea. Mum does."

"Yes, excellent."

This speedy judgement was most unusual for Dad. I wasn't quite convinced that he was being serious.

"Just like that? Don't you want me to tell you any more about it?" I asked him.

He turned to Mum. "I don't believe this daughter of ours. I say to her, 'Go on, tell me more,' and she says, 'There's nothing more to tell.' I say, 'It's an excellent idea,' and she says, 'Don't you want me to tell you any more about it?'"

"Oh, Dad!" Now I was *really* exasperated. "I just need to be sure you're serious because tomorrow I'm going to see Jan with the others, and by next week I could be working."

"What about a work permit?"

Good. This was more like it.

"What do I have to do?"

"Phone the LEA and ask for a form to fill in for a work permit. They'll send you a medical form. I'll give you the number, but first you need to get the OK from Jan."

"I know, that's the difficult bit."

"I can't help you with that. You'll all have to impress her so much that she can't refuse."

"I'm crossing my fingers that all the other parents are as supportive as you two."

"Why? Whose parents do you think won't be?"

"Jaimini's."

"Jaimini Riva?"

"Yes."

"I'm starving."

"Lasagne coming up," Mum said.

"Mm. Smells good."

The conversation seemed to have abruptly moved on from the café, and I was about to leave the kitchen when the phone rang. I answered it. It was Jaimini, sounding really excited, so I went into the sitting room with the phone.

"You'll never guess what, Fen! When I mentioned the café my mum said, 'No, definitely not! There is absolutely nothing more to be said on the subject, and anyway there is no *way* your father will agree.' So I was in the depths of despair till Dad walked in. Well, apparently the train was delayed and he met up with your dad, and your dad persuaded my dad to have a drink with him, and then – and this is the most fantastic bit – your dad managed to convince him that the café was a great idea, and now Dad's managed to persuade Mum, too. It's absolutely incredibly wicked, Fen!"

"Yeah, wicked," I agreed, happily, though that isn't a word I usually use.

We chatted for a while before hanging up, then I went back into the kitchen. Dad was watching TV and drinking coffee with Mum. I crept up behind him, put my hands over his eyes and said, "Guess who?"

"Someone very clumsy who's just spilt my coffee," he answered.

"Sorry," I said, leaping to the sink and grabbing a cloth. "Thanks for working on Jaimini's dad. You're brilliant," I said.

"No problem," he replied with his mouth full.

"I didn't think you knew anything about it till tonight."

"Mum was telling me about it yesterday. We were saying what a shame it would be if it all came to nothing. By the way, I like your way of saying thank you. I was just wanting some coffee tipped down my shirt."

"Take it off, Trev," laughed Mum, as she watched me rubbing away at the coffee stain and making an even bigger mess.

I meant to ask what was up with Rachel before I went to bed, but I completely forgot.

The next day was actually fine for a change. The six of us met up at the end of the netball courts. This is our regular outside meeting place. You can usually rely on privacy at that far end because it's in full view of the staff-room window. That didn't bother us. We weren't doing anything the teachers would disapprove of – just talking.

Luce had pulled a large tissue from her pocket. She spread it out on the ground and showed us a collection of earrings. "Look, these are my favourites," she said, deftly putting on a huge pair of gold loops. Of the six of us, only Luce and Jaimini have pierced ears. Jaimini always wears teeny studs. Even though they are so minute, your eyes are somehow attracted to them. She has four or five different pairs. My favourite pair are the tiniest diamonds in the world. They sparkle and make Jaimini look even more beautiful. She wears them for special occasions only.

"Look, these suit you much better, Luce," Jaimini told her best friend. She gently removed the big gold ones which I secretly thought were hideous, and put on Luce a pair of small silver ones with a tiny black stone in them. As I watched Luce sitting perfectly still, I thought what an odd pair they were to be best friends. Jaimini, so calm with her coffee-cream skin and her intelligent eyes. And Luce quite the opposite – never still – always looking round for something new. Best-friendship was certainly strange. Jaimini had been right. Luce looked ten times better in the silver and black earrings. "Those look great, Luce," Leah told her warmly.

"I'll tell you what I really want," Luce said excitedly, her eyes flashing briefly round our circle. "There are some absolutely brilliant, pull-through earrings in the jeweller's next to the café. They're just long silver strands that you simply pull through, and they're only three ninety-five. I've got that much saved. I must buy them before they go." (You see – there she was, wanting something new.) The next moment the earrings were forgotten.

"Don't look now but Billabong's watching us," Leah said, without moving her lips. Of course we all instantly looked up at the staff-room window. We call him Billabong because his name is William Blundell and he comes from Australia. (Work it out!) He's only about twenty-four. We think this is probably his first job. He teaches technology. Out of the six of us, Leah is the only one who's in his group for tec.

"Lucky thing, Leah. I wish he was my tec teacher. He's really nice-looking," said Luce.

"Stop staring, Luce," Andy told her. The rest of us had only given him a glance but Luce was still transfixed.

Being Luce, she took no notice at all of Andy. Instead she stood right up on tiptoe and waved vigorously to him as though she'd just spotted a long-lost friend in the distance. The funny thing was, Billabong didn't look cross or anything; he just gave a nervous little wave back, then disappeared from view. Five hands grabbed Luce and pulled her down, then we all collapsed in giggles.

When we'd calmed down, we got on with the real business of the meeting. We already knew that everybody's parents were in agreement. We'd established that during assembly through a series of very subtle little eyebrow raises and nods. Of course, we were all on cloud nine.

"I can't believe that my parents are letting me," Jaimini said, for about the tenth time. Then my dad came in for another bucketful of praise. The trouble is that Jaimini is the only one out of all of us who is an only child, so her parents' quota of strictness all goes on her, whereas if she had a brother or sister, half would be used up on them.

Luce, on the other hand, lives with her mum and her stepdad. She has two older half-brothers from her stepdad's first marriage, and two younger half-brothers by her mum and stepdad. She herself is from her mum's first marriage. She quite often visits her dad at weekends, which'll need sorting out carefully when we do the work rota.

Tash's mum and dad are divorced, so Tash lives with her mum, Peta and her brother Danny, who's nearly sixteen. Her mum had agreed quite easily apparently and so had Leah's parents. Leah has got one older sister, aged fifteen, by the way. The only one of the six of us who was rather quiet was Andy. In one way there was nothing strange about that because Andy is usually quiet. But today she seemed really subdued.

"Are you OK, Andy?" Leah asked her best friend.

"Yes, fine," Andy was quick to answer.

"Was it a struggle getting your mum to agree?" Leah pressed her.

"She phoned up Dad in France and they had this great long conversation."

"But they agreed in the end?" Tash asked.

"Yes … they did," Andy said hesitantly.

I knew we all felt sorry for Andy at that moment. There was obviously something wrong. Or maybe she was just upset about her father being away all the time. He works in France which means that Andy and her baby brother hardly ever see him. One of her parents must have given Andy a hard time, because she was keeping very quiet. That was typical. If ever you told Andy a secret, you could guarantee she wouldn't tell another soul. Or if you left your diary or a private letter at her house, you knew she would never dream of reading it. She's just that type of person.

"Right," I said, calling the meeting to attention, "as soon as the end-of-school bell goes, let's go straight to the cloakrooms and brush our hair and tie it back – except Andy, whose hair is only two centimetres long all over, and always looks fantastic anyway…" (She smiled when I said that.)

"What about me?" wailed Luce. "I keep trying to train my hair to tidy itself up, but I'm afraid it doesn't get the message, and right now it's rioting!"

Jaimini produced two lovely silver slides that she sometimes wore in her own hair, and said to Luce, "I thought about your hair this morning and brought these for you."

"Brilliant," said Luce, allowing Jaimini to pull back the front part of her hair on either side into a slide, which made her face look older and more serious.

"Jan is going to think we've got a new girl in our crowd," said Tash.

"Talking of Jan," I continued, "we've got to approach her firmly but politely, assertively but calmly."

"You've not been eating the dictionary again, have you, Fen?" Tash asked.

"I'm quoting my mum," I laughed. "OK, so let's meet outside the main gates of the school and go into town together."

At four o'clock we walked into the café, heads held high but not too high, smart uniform, neat hair, and hearts beating at three hundred and sixty beats per minute.

"Oh, yes, I'd forgotten you were coming today," Jan said, looking not all that pleased to see us. Becky was moving between tables at sixty miles per hour. Louise was nowhere to be seen and Jan looked, and was, fraught.

"May we have a moment of your time?" I asked, trying to sound as grown up as possible.

"Not now, you may not. Surely you can see I'm up to my eyes, Fen."

Oh, dear, this wasn't at all how I'd imagined the conversation going.

"Look, come back later – OK?"

"Yes. When?"

"Six o'clock."

"I've got drama club," hissed Luce in my ear.

"Aha! Problems already, eh?" said Jan, pouncing on Luce's badly-timed confession.

"No problem, I'll miss it," said Luce quick as a flash, which earned her a smile from Jan, who then hurried away with some plates and cups and saucers. I stared at her departing back for a moment, thinking this is not how Jan normally behaves. Is she really so very against us working here? Then I turned and led the way out of the café. The others followed meekly. As we shuffled out I'm sure we all felt the same, like a bunch of silly little girls with big ideas.

We stood outside in a cluster for a few seconds to check that we could all come back at six. Luce insisted that she didn't mind missing drama club and Andy looked worried, but said it would be OK. The others said it was no problem.

Then we parted, three in one direction, three in the other, feeling very downcast and somehow a little foolish.

Chapter 4

"I'm sorry we interrupted you earlier on," I began, tentatively.

"No, I'm the one who's sorry," Jan replied. "I shouldn't have snapped at you."

"You were very busy, though," Tash said to make Jan feel better.

"Yes, I was. Anyway, come and sit down."

We'd arrived at six on the dot, hoping that the punctuality would score us a few points. The front of the café displayed a prominent CLOSED sign and the door was locked. I had given it the very faintest of rattles to check it was really locked, then we had all trooped round the back and knocked timidly on the kitchen door. Without even discussing it, every one of us had kept on our school uniform, which made us look smarter as a group.

Jan had put two tables together in the café itself, and that's where we were now sitting.

"The thing is," she went on, eyeing us thoughtfully one at a time, "Louise went to see about her new job this afternoon, which gave me the perfect opportunity to see how I could manage the café with Becky only."

We nodded understandingly.

"Well, right now I'm nearly on my knees, which proves it's far too much for just two people."

I sat up a little straighter and could feel the rest of the girls doing the same.

"I have to be honest with you, I'm not a hundred per cent happy about taking such young girls on. I need to be certain that you intend to do the job thoroughly and conscientiously."

"We will…" we all murmured.

"Let me remember your names … no,

don't tell me … Tash, I know of course … and you're Jaimini, aren't you?"

"Yes," Jaimini whispered.

We were all behaving as though we'd come face to face with the Pope. I wasn't sure why. Never mind, Luce would soon relax the atmosphere. Good old Luce.

"Now, let me think … yes … you're Leah … the musician," Jan added, and Leah looked down modestly.

Why was no one speaking? This was getting really embarrassing. Jan wasn't going to think we had very much character if we just sat there like dummies. After all, she needed to be sure we'd chat to the customers, didn't she? I decided to give Leah an opening for some conversation.

"Leah's violin lessons are on a Thursday, so we'd have to make sure that fitted in with the rota … and haven't you got orchestral practice one day, Leah?" I asked, brightly.

Jan gave me a look that said "Who rattled your cage?" so I shut up, feeling totally juvenile.

"You're Annie S, aren't you?" Jan went on, with a fair attempt at Andy's real name.

"Most people call me Andy, it's easier," Andy said, with a smile.

"Then Andy it is," Jan said, warmly. "So that leaves Lucy…"

"I hope you might say 'Luce' when you know me better," offered Luce, in her poshest and most demure voice. I couldn't work out what had got into my friends. They were usually so much livelier than this. Jan wasn't going to be able to form any opinion of them if they kept up this "Yes miss, no miss, three bags full miss."

"*If* I decided to take you all on," Jan said, stressing the *if*, "the hours would be from four to six every weekday – we close at five-thirty – and two-thirty to six-thirty on a Saturday, closing at six."

We all nodded like good little girls.

"Yes, I told the others that's what I thought it would be," I put in, cheerfully. This time it was Tash who frowned at me, while Jan just ignored me. I decided to shut up for good.

"This rota you mentioned would have to be sorted out several weeks in advance, and would also have to be absolutely foolproof. I *cannot* be let down."

"That's the good thing about having six of us. If one is ill, then there are five others who can step in," said Leah softly.

"That's a great advantage, of course," Jan replied, "but the trouble starts if you disagree with each other. For example, what if Fen is ill and she phones Tash to cover for her, but Tash is out so she phones Leah and Leah says, 'Yes, that's fine.' Tash might think that's not fair, especially if it's Bank Holiday Monday the next week and Monday should have been *her* day. Also, Leah covered for Andy the previous week so Leah gets more money..."

Jan paused and looked round the table at us. We all stayed silent and wide-eyed. I even began to feel guilty for being ill, as though all that Jan was saying had actually happened.

"I want you to be aware of the sort of problems that may arise, that's all. Now, I'm going to make a cup of tea for all of us while you put your heads together and come up with a rota which starts next week – the week beginning Monday 6th October. You can work out six weeks."

Jan thrust a huge sheet of paper on the table along with a few sheets of rough paper and handed a pen to Jaimini. For the next five minutes she hummed to herself as she pottered about making the tea and tidying up, while we worked away at the rota. Never had our school work or homework been done with as much care and attention as we were giving this. Nobody spoke above a whisper and we just kept trying things out, then scrapping them when they didn't work. It was much more complicated than we had thought it would be, because of all the clubs and sports practices and classes we did between the six of us, and because of wanting to rotate the Saturdays. Eventually, we came up with this and showed it to Jan:

Week beginning 6th Oct

- Mon — Fen
- Tues — Leah
- Wed — Tash
- Thurs — Jaimes
- Fri — Andy
- Sat — Luce

Week beginning 13th Oct

- Mon — Luce
- Tues — Leah
- Wed — Tash
- Thurs — Jaimes
- Fri — Andy
- Sat — Fen

Week beginning 20th Oct

- Mon — Luce
- Tues — Fen
- Wed — Tash
- Thurs — Jaimes
- Fri — Andy
- Sat — Leah

Week beginning 27th Oct

- Mon — Luce
- Tues — Fen
- Wed — Leah
- Thurs — Jaimes
- Fri — Andy
- Sat — Tash

Week beginning 3rd Nov

- Mon — Luce
- Tues — Fen
- Wed — Leah
- Thurs — Tash
- Fri — Andy
- Sat — Jaimes

Week beginning 10th Nov

- Mon — Luce
- Tues — Fen
- Wed — Leah
- Thurs — Tash
- Fri — Jaimes
- Sat — Andy

Jan spent ages staring at it. She also looked at our rough plans. The kitchen was as silent as an empty church. Finally when we thought she'd never put it down, she did, with the words, "I'm impressed. Well done!" We all relaxed our hunched shoulders and beamed round at each other as though we'd just been told we'd passed our French oral exam. I say French oral on purpose because the only one of us who didn't look all that happy and relieved was Andy (and, of course, she wouldn't if it was a French exam because she speaks fluent French anyway, so it would be no big deal). I couldn't work Andy out, but pushed it to the back of my mind till later, then listened to what Jan was going on to say.

"The next thing to do is to get work permits from the LEA." We all wrote down the telephone number. "Get your mums to help you fill in the form, and there'll be a medical form to fill in as well, but you all look quite healthy to me." She grinned round at us. She was right, we were a healthy bunch. For no particular reason, except that I was feeling happy, I gave Tash a special smile. Perhaps I was being over-sensitive but I could have sworn she went pink. She certainly looked down, I didn't imagine that. I guess she was probably feeling like I was earlier on – guilty for being ill when she wasn't even ill.

"Once the work permits are signed and the rota has been double-checked and you've worked out and agreed the plan for last minute cover of someone's duty, you're free to start. Incidentally, no one has asked me how much you'll be earning. I thought that was the whole point of the exercise."

Not one of us spoke. Personally, I'd completely forgotten about the money. It came as a sudden nice surprise.

"Put it this way, you're not going to become millionaires overnight," Jan said, with a smile. "I can pay you two pounds sixty-five pence an hour, at the moment."

Little smiles whizzed round the table. It was all sounding so real now.

"And for that I expect hard work. I can tell from the way you've all been so sensible and let me do the talking at this meeting that I don't need to tell you you must always be polite and pleasant to customers, and don't chat unless they lead you into a chat. Even then you have to be able to keep it limited without appearing rude."

So, *that* was it. The others had judged it better than I had. I had thought Jan would be looking for bubbly, lively girls and she was actually looking for girls who could keep quiet. I cupped my cheeks in my hands so the blush wouldn't show.

"One other thing – I think it's best if you wear your school uniforms without the sweaters. Black skirt and white shirt is absolutely fine and I'll provide you with an apron. You're on three weeks trial from when we start on the sixth of October. That gives us next week to sort out work permits. I'd also like you come in next week on the same day that you'll be doing when you start properly, to get a bit of practice. I'll be there to show you where we keep things and so on. But I warn you, a large part of the work will be boring washing up in the kitchen."

We all nodded.

"The three week trial is for you as much as for me, so that if you don't like the work for any reason, you can tell me, and we can reconsider. Don't forget there's no shortage of people to fill the vacancy if you lot don't come up to scratch."

She cast a warning eye round all of us.

"We won't let you down, Jan," Jaimini said.

"No, we won't," the rest of us murmured.

"No, somehow I don't think you will," Jan said, looking directly at Jaimini with a frank, warm look.

For some reason or other I felt a little pang of jealousy at that moment. I knew it was stupid, because after all I wanted us to get the job all together, yet somehow I felt as though the others were becoming just as important to Jan as I was, which didn't seem fair as I started it all off *and* I'm her niece. It was only a little pang of jealousy and I didn't like myself for feeling it, but I couldn't help it.

That was the precise moment that Jan

suddenly said, "Right, meeting over. Now we can all relax. I'm off home and so should you be, but first I want a chat with one of my favourite nieces," and she put her hand out towards me and gave a tiny jerk of the head as if to say come and sit over here by me.

A lovely warm feeling came over me and completely swamped that little pang of jealousy.

"Happy now, pet?" she asked.

I just nodded. I had learnt something important that day: I had to keep the fact that I was Jan's niece completely separate from the café job. All the time I was working for her she was my employer, then as soon as I'd finished she was my aunt again.

Later, at home, in our kitchen, Mum and Dad listened to my story of our interview.

"Yes, she's a real businesswoman, your sister," said Dad to Mum. "She's a lot less stupid than she looks."

Mum gave him a friendly cuff and said, "You leave my sister alone. Nobody's stupid in my family!"

It was quite late. Rachel and Emmy had already gone to bed so it was a shock to hear the kitchen door suddenly click open. Our kitchen door has a strong catch on it. It can't open on its own.

"Emmy?" Mum said. There was no reply. I saw Dad frown slightly. We all kept our eyes on the door as it opened very slowly. There, standing like a ghost in the doorway, still and pale in her long white nightie, stood Rachel.

"I hate you," she said, staring straight ahead of her.

My heart was really beating. I thought she must have been sleepwalking. I saw an angry look appear on Dad's face but before he could say anything, Mum spoke in a very ordinary voice.

"Do you want a drink, Rachel?"

"No, I just came to tell Fen I hate her for what she's done to me."

Mum didn't sound quite so normal now.

"What's going on, Fen?" she asked me in a serious voice.

"I've no idea," I answered, shakily.

"I'll be back in a minute." Mum took Rachel by the hand and led her back to bed.

Dad and I waited in the kitchen. I felt like a criminal.

"What's she talking about, Fen?" Dad asked me in his most serious tone as soon as they'd gone.

"I wish I knew, but I honestly haven't got the faintest idea."

After that we sat in uncomfortable silence till Mum came back. I could tell Dad didn't believe me. And then when Mum *did* come back things got worse.

"Why did you ruin Rachel's dress, Fen?"

My mouth formed an O of surprise but not a sound came out. I was speechless. "I can't believe it of you," she went on. My speech came back. I was cross.

"Look, Mum, I never touched her stupid dress. She's making it up to get at me because I've got the café job."

"She doesn't even know about the café job," snapped Mum.

"Look, Mum, I swear I don't even know

which dress you're talking about."

"Her favourite dress. It's been cut all the way round above the hem. It was only just long enough for Rachel before, but it's definitely too short now, and she loved that dress."

I looked at Dad for help. "I didn't cut it, honestly Dad."

His face looked like a thundercloud. I wasn't going to get any help there. I suddenly had a burst of inspiration.

"It must have been Emmy."

Mum and Dad looked at each other, considering the possibility.

"So you're saying it definitely wasn't you?" Dad asked, carefully.

"I'm saying that I swear on the Holy Bible, cross my heart and hope to die, I did not cut any dresses. Promise and double promise."

"Well, OK," Mum said, hesitantly. She gave me her best shot at a smile but it was lopsided and strange. It was obvious she still wasn't totally convinced.

"You'd better go to bed, Fen. It's very late."

I jumped up but stopped by the door.

"Oh, just one thing, Mum, Jan wants us to have a trial week next week, each of us helping in the café on the same day as when the rota really starts. That means I'm the first one – Monday…"

"I'm not making any promises at the moment," Mum said, quietly. "I want this thing with Rachel sorted out. She's absolutely heartbroken up there. Anyway, there's one thing that puzzles me."

"What?" I asked, feeling my own heart slipping downwards towards the region of my socks.

"Emmy couldn't have cut the dress because it's been done with the pinking shears, which are quite heavy compared to the ordinary scissors. I find them awkward myself, so she'd certainly never manage such a straight line. No, it wasn't Emmy who cut Rachel's dress."

I looked at Mum in horror. There was nothing more I could say.

"I've told you it wasn't me," I repeated in a whisper, then I went upstairs to bed with heavy slow steps.

* * *

The next morning was sunny. It always gave me a happy feeling to wake up to sunshine, but this morning the happy feeling was instantly squashed by a cold bleak feeling.

We sat round that breakfast table like a family whose treasured old cat had just died or something. All except Emmy who prattled on and on and didn't even notice the terrible atmosphere. I didn't look at Rachel once, she made me so mad. If she was trying to stop me having the café job then she was succeeding because Mum and Dad were not happy with me.

That dress had been given to our family about three months before by an old friend of Mum's called Felicity. Felicity has a very good job, pots of money and no family of her own. She was just passing through England on her way back to America. She had picked the dress up in London and said she simply couldn't resist it. She had wrapped it up and handed it to Mum with two other wrapped gifts. One was very obviously for Emmy but the other could have been for Rachel *or* me. It was a Game Boy.

We're not a particularly technical family. Even though we have to do loads of computer work at school, I'm one of the only kids in the class who hasn't got a computer at home and doesn't really want one. Rachel and I both quite liked the idea of the Game Boy, but we both definitely wanted the dress, which was surprising because I'm always in leggings or jeans, and Rachel's usually in jeans or cycling shorts. I tell you, that dress was brilliant, even though it was so simple. It was very dark green with wide shoulders, a slightly scooped neck and short sleeves. It came in at the waist, then flared right out.

I'm only just thirteen and Rachel's very nearly ten, plus I'm quite small for my age and Rachel's on the tall side, so the dress fitted both of us, though it was a bit longer on her.

"Who's it for? Who's it for?" Rachel and I had both asked Mum, frantically, and she had searched every scrap of wrapping paper, including the paper round Emmy's present, for any clue as to which of us Felicity had intended to have the dress. I even found a dark blue squiggle on the wrapping paper that looked just like an F for Fen, but then Rachel found another that could have been an R.

"There's nothing for it, I shall just have to phone her," Mum said, with an exasperated sigh, and she did.

Felicity's world shattering answer was that she didn't know which one of us would fit the dress, or even like it, so she had decided to leave the decision with Mum. With that she had gaily put the phone down, not realizing that she had left Mum with World War Three to sort out.

In the end she tossed a coin. Rachel won. I was very disappointed for about two days but then I got over it, especially as Mum said that for Christmas she'd try to get me something similar. In fact, Rachel had asked me to try it on again a few days ago and I must have grown even in that short time because it was too short for me. Rachel herself had never actually worn the dress. Well, she'd worn it round the house but she'd never really had anything appropriate to wear it to – until now.

She had been invited to a disco at her best friend Jenny's house. Jenny lives in quite a big house and she was having fifteen people to her party, lucky thing.

So, there we were eating our silent breakfast (apart from Emmy's little bursts of nonsense) when Mum suddenly got up, marched over to the kitchen drawer and got out the pinking shears and a scrap of material. She handed them both to Emmy.

"Can you cut that material, Emmy? Have a try."

All eyes watched with interest as Emmy grinned round at us, enjoying being the centre of attention. She picked up the very large scissors clumsily, her mouth open in concentration, her eyes wide with excitement. Even Dad had lowered his newspaper and was waiting to see what happened. Emmy was showing no sign of ever having seen, let alone used, this strange utensil. She got her fingers and thumb in place, but because the handle of the shears was so big the other end kept falling down. Finally she managed to open the scissors and took aim with the sharp end, but they just folded the material awkwardly and didn't cut at all. She got fed up in the end.

"Too big," she told Mum, leaving them at the side of her plate while the material dropped to the floor and she got on with her toast. I looked at Rachel. Were those tears in her eyes?

"Can I get ready for school, Mum?" I asked, wanting to get away from the awful atmosphere.

"Yes, go on," she said, a touch briskly.

Yet another wet break. I didn't feel like chatting. The six of us were sitting in Jaimini's and Luce's registration room. The others were all talking excitedly about next week. Tash, Leah, Jaimini and Luce had all persuaded their mums to get the work permits organized that very day – Friday.

I said I'd forgotten all about it. Tash looked at me in amazement and said, "You forgot?

How could you?" I tried to look unconcerned and said, "Oh, I expect Mum will organize it, we just didn't mention it, that's all. Anyway if she forgets we can do it on Monday." I grinned but I was feeling really sick inside and wanted to get away from the other five. I didn't even want to tell Tash about the dress because I couldn't tell her without sounding horrible about Rachel, and as much as I hated her guts at that moment, I still felt a strong sense of family loyalty towards her, and something told me all was not quite as it seemed…

"I'm just going back to the classroom. I'll be back in a few minutes," I said as casually as I could. Only Leah realized there was anything the matter with me. Nothing escapes Leah. She mouthed, "You OK?" I nodded and smiled, then slipped away. The others didn't see. They were absorbed in their own conversation.

People kept bumping into me all the way down the corridor. Why don't they look where they're going? I wondered a bit crossly, then I realized that I was the one who wasn't looking. I'd been miles away thinking about Rachel.

"Fen, Fen!"

Who was that? I turned round to see Andy struggling along the corridor. There were seven hundred and fifty pupils in our school and just then it seemed like they were all in this one corridor. Andy's cropped head kept bobbing in and out of view. Finally she bobbed right up to me. I must confess I didn't really want company at that moment, but as soon as I saw the expression on her face I forgot my own problems.

"What's the matter, Andy?"

"Can I talk to you?"

"Yeah, course."

There's a covered way just outside the year-ten classrooms and we went out there. We stood shoulders hunched and arms tightly folded, shivering in the narrow dry bit, surrounded by pelting rain and distorted background noises of kids laughing and shrieking. The rain fell and fell making brittle little thumps and twangs on all the different surfaces. Sometimes it blocked out the voices of all the raucous pupils still careering about in the real world away from us, sometimes it muffled them. My own voice, when I spoke, sounded thin and shaky.

"What's the matter?" I asked Andy again. Her usually dark skin looked paler, her usually big eyes looked even bigger.

"I'm not allowed," she said in scarcely more than a whisper.

"Not allowed to what?" I asked, though I knew the answer really.

"To do the café job."

"Why?"

She answered with another statement.

"But I'm doing it anyway."

"What?!"

And another statement.

"Because I can't let you all down."

"How?"

"I've worked it all out. Don't tell the others, Fen. I know how badly you all want this to work, and if I drop out, the rota will be impossible, and Jan will immediately think,

'Oh, yeah, that's one. When will the others follow suit?'"

"But Andy, what about…?"

"The work permit? I've thought about that. Get your mum to get the forms for me, too. Say that my mum asked if she would because my mum's French and she wasn't sure how to go about it. Your mum'll believe that…"

"But *your* mum'll have to sign it."

"I'm going to forge her signature. I've already practised it."

(I told you Andy was daring; well, this is what I meant.)

"Andy, you could get in real trouble for doing that. And what if someone sees you working in the café and tells your mum?"

"I'll cross that bridge when I come to it. Go on, Fen. At least ask your mum to get me the form."

"I don't even know if Mum's going to get the form for *me*. I'm in deep trouble at home for something I didn't even do."

"What?" asked Andy.

So there we stood till the end of break. I

explained the dress saga to Andy from beginning to end. As I talked and she listened, I was aware of the rain getting heavier and slanting in towards us. Our hair was sticking to our faces however much we kept to the covered way. Neither of us cared. We were two girls, each with a big problem, and a friend to share it with.

By the end of break I knew what I was going to do. Andy had given me her opinion. It had alarmed me. We'd also worked out how to tackle her problem. It seemed it was actually her father in France who disagreed with the café idea, and he'd told her mother that on no account should she allow Andy to go ahead with it. Andy reckoned her mother would have let her do it if it had been left up to her. We decided to tackle her mother over the weekend, perhaps with the help of my mum, but first I had to sort out my own problem.

I was worried sick about the whole dress episode, but I was innocent and that's a great driver. I couldn't wait for the school day to roll on so I could get home.

Chapter 5

"Mum, you know that dress…" I began as soon I walked in through the back door.

"It's OK," Mum said, putting an arm round my shoulders. "I know it wasn't you."

"It was…"

"Rachel."

"Yes."

We stood looking at each other for a few seconds. I couldn't believe that such a big problem had been ironed out in a conversation of so few words. But then I realized that of course it hadn't been ironed out, because there must have been something terribly wrong with Rachel for her to completely ruin one of her most precious possessions and then to pin the blame on me.

Thinking back, she'd been setting it up for the last few days. I'd noticed it – all the nasty meaningful comments – but I'd put it to the back of my mind each time because of the café job being so much more important. Little did I realize that this was actually the more important of the two because it almost destroyed my chances of the café job.

"Why did she do it?" I asked, simply.

"That I don't know."

"Well, how can you be sure it *was* her, then?"

"Because a) it was totally out of character for you to do something so malicious, and b) you've never been any good at telling lies. I also knew that Emmy wasn't involved because she couldn't manage the pinking shears at all and she didn't go red or anything when I asked her to try out some cutting."

"Did Rachel confess straight away when you tackled her?"

"Yes, more or less, because I went in heavy. It was the only way. I just said 'Rachel, I know you cut that dress yourself and I want you to tell me why.'"

"What did she say?"

"She burst into tears and said, 'I can't tell you why. You won't understand and you'll think I'm stupid.' I've done everything I can to try to calm her down and get her to tell me, but it's no good. Why don't you go up and see her? She's in her room. She's been up there all day."

"She didn't go to school?"

"No."

"Where's Emmy?"

"She's staying for tea at Alice Bainbridge's."

So up I went. I decided to change out of my school uniform first. I pushed open my bedroom and just stood there staring.

Hanging from one corner of my room right across to the one diagonally opposite was a huge message. Each letter of the message had been cut out of an A4 pad and carefully coloured in. The letters were all hanging from a long piece of green ribbon. They didn't flutter. They didn't move at all. The message was beautifully clear. It read:

I'M SORRY, FEN. PLEASE FORGIVE ME.

I didn't bother to change at all. I just went straight into Rachel's room. She was sitting at her desk with her back to me.

"I forgive you," I said from the door, and she turned round to face me with a terribly pale, blotchy face and swollen eyes. Her body was still doing those big silent sobs that you can't help doing if you've been really crying for a long time. I suddenly had a picture of Andy and me talking and talking and getting soaked without caring. I remembered what Andy had said.

"Rachel," I said, sitting down on her bed and patting the space next to me for her to sit down. "Were you going to wear that dress for Jenny's disco?"

"Yes," she said, uncertainly.

Now I would see if Andy had been right.

"You don't want to go to the disco, do you?"

Her eyes darted from side to side while she struggled to decide whether to tell me.

"No," she said finally.

I was about to ask her why not, but I stopped myself just in time because that would have been too much for her to answer, so instead I said, "Did you think if you ruined your dress you'd have the perfect excuse not to go?"

"Yes," she answered, in hardly more than a whisper.

"Is it something to do with Jenny, why you don't want to go?"

A long pause and another silent sob. I waited.

"Yes."

"Has she really upset you?"

"Mm."

"Isn't she your best friend any more?"

"I'm not *her* best friend any more." This was so mumbled I hardly heard it, but at least she'd given me some information, not just a yes or a no, so I pushed a little harder.

"Why not?"

There was such a long pause before she spoke again that I began to think she mustn't have heard me. When at last she did speak her voice got louder and angrier the more she said, and she nearly cried again.

"She's got a new best friend now, called Natalie. She's very pretty and I hate her. I can't go to Jenny's if Nattyknickers is going to be there," Rachel said, looking dangerously close to tears again.

I had a job not laughing when she said that so seriously. "Is it because you're jealous of Natalie taking your best friend from you?"

Rachel suddenly came out with a great long speech.

"And also because of the dog. Jenny's dog is a German shepherd and Jenny's mum always lets it romp around wherever it wants and I just can't bear it. I'd scream if it came near me, and yesterday Jenny and Natalie spent ages making fun of me about my fear of dogs. Jenny started imitating what I do when I go to her house. Gnat's Poo fell about laughing and in her stupid American accent she said, 'Oh, gee, that's real sad, Jenny. How can you have such a dingbat for a best friend?' "

I hated Natalie before I'd even met her. "Is she American, then?"

"Yes, and I wish she'd go back there."

"Is she going to be in this country for long?"

"Till next summer. Her dad works for the government in a very important job."

"Couldn't you talk to Jenny on her own some time? Tell her she's making you really unhappy?"

"She's still nice to me in school because Natalie isn't there, but she never wants to play with me after school because that's when she plays with Natalie."

"How does she know Natalie, then?"

"From ballet. I went to meet Jenny after ballet last week, like I often do, but I'll never ever do that again because Natalie wouldn't even let me talk to Jenny. She said, 'Go away. Jenny's *my* best friend now, aren't you Jenny?' "

"What did Jenny say?"

"She looked at the ground and said 'yes', so I walked home on my own."

I was just about to say something like, "Well, stuff her then. Get yourself another best friend," when I thought about me and Tash. We'd had a massive fall out a couple of years before and I'd gone round saying all sorts of nasty things about her. Of course we made it up later and I felt horribly guilty about all the awful things I'd said, so I didn't want to encourage Rachel to make the same mistake.

"One thing I don't understand is why you went to such lengths to get out of going to the party. Why didn't you just explain to Mum?"

"Mum wouldn't understand. She'd think I was stupid and then she'd make me go anyway. I know the idea about cutting the dress was crazy, but I felt as if I *was* crazy. I even began to believe *myself* that it was you who had cut the dress. In fact I even made Emmy believe it. You must really hate me. I hate myself."

Rachel suddenly looked very afraid. She gripped my arm so tightly it hurt.

"You won't tell anyone I cut the dress, will you? I mean, not a single person. Promise me you won't mention the dress to another living soul."

"OK, OK, I promise," I said, while trying to prise her fingers off my arm. I surreptitiously rubbed the indentations from her tight clasp for the next couple of minutes.

"There's one other thing I don't understand, Rachel." She eyed me anxiously. "Why did you tell me that Tash said I could phone back any time, when she stressed to both you and Emmy that she wanted me to call back the moment I walked through the door?"

Rachel's pale face turned even paler. "It was all part of trying to be horrible to you. I wanted Mum and Dad to really believe I hated you."

"But Mum and Dad didn't even know about Tash's phone call."

"No, but Emmy did, and I hoped she might tell them."

I nodded, but I was puzzled. Something just wasn't adding up. I mean, surely *nobody* could dread going to a party so much that they would go to the lengths that Rachel had gone to, to get out of it. I was about to press my point when I saw how crumpled and sad her face looked. I decided she'd had enough interrogation for now.

"Come on," I said, heaving her to her feet, "let's go down to Mum. She'll help you sort everything out. You don't know Mum very well if you think she'd make you go to a party you dreaded going to."

She didn't argue, just followed me meekly down to the kitchen and sat down. I quickly told Mum the problem and she sat Rachel on her knee and said, "Listen, love, I know you won't get much comfort from this at the moment, but all I can say is that *real* best friends don't just stop being best friends unless the friendship wasn't all that good in the first place. So just be patient, and Jenny will soon get tired of the novelty of Natalie. If she doesn't, then you know you're probably better off with a different best friend. But all best friends quarrel occasionally."

"I'm not waiting till next summer when Nattypants goes back to America," Rachel said with great feeling.

"No, of course not," Mum agreed, trying not to smile, "just wait a few weeks…"

"A few weeks!" Rachel exploded.

Poor Rachel. A few weeks seemed quite a long time even to me, so to her it must have seemed a lifetime. I said something I was quite proud of then.

"You don't actually have to *wait*, Rachel. Carry on as normal as though you don't care at all what she does. She'll soon change her tune then."

Rachel's back straightened and her chin lifted. Mum and I exchanged the teeniest of looks. It was going to be OK now.

"Right, come on, we all need some fresh air. Let's go out for a walk on the common."

Rachel hesitated but only for a second. I knew why. It was because she was worried about the dogs on the common. She'd been bitten by a collie when she was about five and she'd been scared of dogs ever since. She'd never go to the common on her own, but as long as she was with someone who knew about her fear, she could cope.

It was a windy day and the sun kept appearing in quick bright flashes. I like that sort of weather. We didn't see a single dog, which was quite unusual, so it was a lovely walk. On the way we picked up Emmy from Alice Bainbridge's house, then I persuaded Mum to call in at Andy's. Andy lived on the other side of the common, two or three streets away, so Emmy was getting quite whiney by the time we got there. I began to regret my suggestion. On the other hand, Mum was keen to make it up to me for having wrongly accused me, so I decided it was a good idea to strike while the iron was hot.

"Come in, pleesse," said Andy's mum, trying not to look too shocked at the sight of the Brooks family *en masse* on her doorstep. I liked her French accent. It suited her. We started taking our mucky shoes off.

"No, no pleeesse, it doesn't matter," Mrs Sorrell assured us, but Mum insisted.

"We don't want to traipse mud through your house," she said.

Mrs Sorrell looks just like Andy, only more, if you know what I mean. Her eyes are even bigger and darker, her hair is very short and wispy and looks as though someone has sculpted it on to her head. Her skin is darker than Andy's and she's got very strong bone structure. Her cheeks cave right in. I've decided to try to get into the habit of sucking my cheeks in and sitting with my knuckles pressing my cheek bones upwards. After a few years I might have lovely hollow cheeks and high cheek bones like Mrs Sorrell.

As well as being really pretty she also looked very smart. She was wearing a tight linen skirt and a crisp, navy blue blouse. Her waist is the littlest waist I've ever seen on a lady.

"Come and seet down, Meesees…?"

"Call me Dee."

"And I am Dominique."

"We were just passing by on our walk and

Fen suggested we popped in and said hello, but do say if it's not a convenient moment, we don't want to disturb you."

You liar, Mum, I thought affectionately.

Andy appeared with her little brother who is just starting to toddle. He was wearing nothing but a nappy which was slowly sliding down, and a bib which was back to front. He was carrying a half-eaten rusk. He tottered over to Mum with a very determined look on his face, and scraped the rusk all down Mum's light blue jeans. It left a revolting long brown trail. We all laughed including Mum. Dominique looked really worried though. Crouching down neatly beside Mum, she began dabbing away with a J-cloth.

"It doesn't matter one bit," said Mum, as she grabbed the J-cloth and finished off with a quick rub.

"He's such a little *cornichon*," Dominique said, eyeing her little boy with that I'm-pretending-to-be-cross look that lots of fond mothers give their children.

"What's *cornichon* in English?" I asked

Andy in a whisper.

"Gherkin," she answered, and we both tried not to laugh.

"Come on, Gherkin," Emmy said, stretching out her hand and trying to look motherly. She didn't realize that not everything French translates into English. "Gherkin, Gherkin," she called in an encouraging sing-song voice. "Come with Emmy." Then she patted her knees and stuck out two hands. Rachel joined in with Andy's and my laughter, though I'm not sure she knew why we were laughing.

Gherkin – or Sebastien (pronounced nearly the same as in English) which is his real name – ignored Emmy completely and tottered off at a rate of knots towards the stairs. We all followed him. Rachel seemed much happier. Sebastien let her pick him up and he tried to stuff the rest of his disgusting rusk up her nose, which brought on another burst of hysterics from me and Andy.

"Let's go in here," Andy suggested, opening a door which led into a massive room full of toys, lots of bean bags, a big red Postman Pat van, and even a computer.

Andy's dad must earn an awful lot of money, I was thinking. And though half of me thought, lucky Andy, the other half thought, but what's the point if he's hardly ever at home? We stayed in the playroom for about half an hour. Andy and I were trying to hear what Mum and Dominique were saying, but the little ones were making so much noise it was impossible.

"Agnès," Dominique called out, eventually. "Do you and Fen want to come in here a moment?" We crossed our fingers, gabbled a quick prayer to the playroom ceiling and went.

"Leesen, *bibiche*," Dominique said to Andy. "You know that your father made eet quite clear that he doesn't want you to do the café job?"

"Ye-es," Andy answered.

"Well, I have talked now with Dee, and I theenk he would like you to do theese job if he understood that eet is only for a very short time each time, and your school work ees not suffering."

"Yes, but surely you said all that to him on the phone…"

"Yes, yes I did, but you know your father, Andy."

A sort of helpless smile passed between Andy and her mum. "So what I theenk is, you do your job for a leetle while, let's say a few weeks, and slowly I weel tell you father that he deed not have to worry after all, because your school work ees fine. Of course, we must be sure you do your school work extra well, hein, *bibiche*?"

Andy's face began to beam. "Yes, I'll do the most brilliant work in the whole class."

Then she turned to me. "We've done it, Fen!" I held out my two palms and she slapped them. Loads of older boys did that at school. I don't know why Andy and I did it at that moment, but we did!

Andy also rushed over to her mum and hugged her, then she gave my mum a hug too and said, "Thanks, Mrs Brooks."

"Don't thank me, it's entirely your mum's decision, and also – call me Dee."

Later, Mum and I discussed the work permits and Mum said she'd already organized mine, as soon as she'd found out that it wasn't me who'd cut the dress. She'd also told Dominique the LEA number so she could phone on Monday.

"I can't wait till Monday," I told Mum, hugging my knees.

"Remember you won't be earning any money."

"Yes, I know but it'll make it all seem more real."

"You need to observe as much as you can," she said, "and be prepared to do a lot of donkey work."

The weekend was never ending, except of course that eventually it did end, and I went to school on Monday morning feeling really excited and happy.

During the day, the excitement melted and the happiness got eaten up by a big burst of nervousness, so that by the time I walked into the kitchen of the café, my knees were knocking and my stomach felt like a tumble drier.

"I'll put my bag down here, shall I, Jan?" I asked timidly, whereas normally I would have just put it down without asking.

"Yes, that's fine. Here, put this apron on." She handed me a whiter-than-white soft apron, which I put on in fear and trepidation, already imagining jam and tea stains all over it.

"Don't look so worried, pet. No one's going to eat you, not unless they get desperate because the food's so bad, anyway!"

My knees stopped trembling when she said that, and a very determined feeling came into my head and swam through every vein in my body. I've had that feeling before. Mum says I'm single-minded. That means that if I want something I go for it, and nothing stops me. For the next hour or so I didn't concentrate on anything except the job in hand.

"What should I do first?"

"I'm going to show you how to load the dishwasher. Then I'm going to explain the table numbering and show you where everything is. I'm leaving you and Becky to hold the fort," she added to Louise, who had just pushed through the swing doors looking harrassed. A strand of hair had fallen out of her bun and was clinging to her face which showed she was sweating.

After about thirty-five minutes I was sweating too. It was partly the heat and partly the hard work. Mum was right about that!

"Avoid contact with customers at first, Fen, just get to know the layout of the tables and where everything is, and do any washing-up that Kevin or the girls ask you to do."

During the first few minutes a very old and frail-looking man had beckoned me over while I was in the middle of clearing and wiping a table on Louise's instructions, after some customers had left.

"'Scuse me, miss," he had called in a quavery voice. I immediately looked round for one of the others but typically there was no one in sight. Jan had said no contact with customers but I could hardly ignore the poor old man.

"'Scuse me," he called out, craning his neck round even more because he had his back to me. I thought he was going to fall out of his chair so I bolted straight over to him, deciding to suffer the consequences if Jan wasn't happy. I put on my best smile, and was about to say, "Yes sir, how may I help you?" (which I'd heard on television in restaurants, banks, building societies, airports etc., etc., goodness knows how many times), when Jan's voice hissed into the back of my neck, "I thought I said no contact with customers."

It wouldn't have been very nice for the old man to know that I had only turned up with such speed because I thought he was about to fall on the floor; on the other hand I wanted Jan to know that I wasn't just blatantly ignoring her orders, so I hissed back at her without moving my lips, like a pretty bad ventriloquist, "I had to come – the old man was desperate."

One or two customers from nearby tables must have heard me because I was aware of amused glances. My face started to go pink. Meanwhile the old man, who I think was a bit deaf, was sort of poking the menu with a stubby finger and mumbling on about muffins or something. Jan, who had got entirely the wrong idea because I had used the word desperate, pushed me and my glowing pink face to one side and heaved the old man to his feet saying. "That's right, love, up you get. The loos are over here."

He was still going on about muffins and looked most surprised to be yanked to his feet like that. I thought I'd better intervene.

"He doesn't want the loo," I hissed at Jan through gritted teeth, which made several customers collapse into their coffees, and turned my face to tomato red.

"You said he was desperate!" she hissed back.

"I only meant desperate for me to go over to him!"

Throughout this, Jan's arms had been

supporting the old man, but as soon as I said that, she just let go and he began to wobble dangerously. A lady from the next table who must have thought he was going to topple right over, leapt up and grabbed the old man. In the process she knocked into her own table and her teacup wobbled in its saucer, then tipped up, pouring tea over half the tablecloth and sending a little stream down the side which trickled on to the floor.

Coincidentally, Louise was walking past the other side of the table at the precise moment when the tea tipped up. The woman, looking more than indignant, said, "That was rather clumsy of you."

"But it wasn't..." Louise began, then obviously remembered what Jan so often told us all – "Remember the customer is always right." In this case the customer was definitely not right, and what's more I think she knew it, which didn't endear her to me one little bit.

Louise shut her mouth and went to get a cloth. She came back with two and handed one to me. I was grateful to be able to busy myself with something instead of standing there with a tomato for a face.

Jan sat the old man down and apologized to him. Louise showed the lady to another table.

"Bring this lady's bags please, Fen," she said to me as though it was an everyday request and nothing unusual had happened. I found the courage to look subtly around and felt relieved because no one was taking any notice any more.

"It wasn't your fault, you know," said the lady when I gave her her bags. "You shouldn't have been left on your own in the first place," she added.

"Oh, I think Mrs Geeson was busy..." I began, trying to defend Jan in my politest tone.

"I'm not talking about her. No – that other one – that Louise. She saw that old man call you, then she just deliberately walked out. I saw it all."

I didn't know what to say, so I pretended to be smoothing out the tablecloth which didn't need smoothing at all. A little while later Jan stopped me in the kitchen.

"Fen," she said with a serious expression.

I was aware of Kevin taking in the whole thing. He was no doubt stocking up material for taking the mickey out of me later about the telling off I was about to receive. I forced my eyes to meet Jan's.

"Yes," I said.

"That old man episode…"

"Yes."

Then her face grew into a big grin and her eyes watered as she let out a great peal of laughter, and gulping air, managed to stutter, "Wasn't it the funniest thing ever?"

From behind me came a massive explosion. I turned round. Becky and Kevin were leaning against each other, helpless with laughter. I couldn't help joining in.

"Becky and I had ringside seats," Kevin spluttered, "through a crack in the door."

"Oh, dear me," said Jan, wiping the tears from her eyes as her last few giggles came out. "Back to work, I suppose."

I learnt so much that first Monday evening. At the end of it I felt tired but happy. I liked all the people I worked with, and it was good to know we could joke and laugh amongst the serious business of running the café.

When everyone had finally gone and the CLOSED sign was firmly in place, and we'd cleared and swept and wiped and vacuumed till the place was sparkling, only then did we sit down and have a cup of tea ourselves. We also had another laugh about the old man episode and even re-enacted it. Kevin had gone so I played the part of the old man. Jan and Louise played themselves and Becky played me. It sent us into further peals of laughter.

"I'm quite sad to be leaving now," Louise said. "It's livening up a bit now Fen's here."

I thought about the café all the way home. I still had my homework to do, but only one subject to be handed in the next day. I began to run, not so that I could get on with my homework, more because I couldn't wait to tell my family all about my first stint in the café. I smiled to myself as I ran. When I was almost home a picture of that lady's face – the one whose bags I'd taken over – came into my head. Where had I seen that face before? I didn't know it then, but that question was going to plague me for quite a while.

Chapter 6

During the rest of that week the others all experienced the same nervous excitement that I had felt on Monday. I think Andy was probably in the worst state of us all because she spent the entire weekend expecting to be told at any moment that she wasn't allowed to do the job at all. We nearly altered the whole rota so that she could do an earlier day and get it over with, but in the end we decided it was better to keep it as it was.

On Friday morning break we were all assembled in our usual place at the far end of the netball courts. Luce was giving us a running commentary on what she thought she could see through the staffroom window, which was very little from that distance. But Luce's imagination was vivid, and what she couldn't see she made up.

"Look! Huh! I never knew Miss Skelton smoked!"

We all dutifully looked.

"It's the steam from someone's coffee," Tash said, rolling her eyes.

"You can't see steam from here," Luce objected.

"You can't see anything from here," retorted Tash, "so it's just as likely to be steam as smoke."

"Oh, no! It's Billabong!"

We didn't even bother to turn round.

"Luce, be quiet, we want to hear about Jaimini's evening at the café."

"But he's opening the window."

"Go on Jaimini, just ignore Luce."

Jaimini had scarcely drawn breath when a great bellow from the direction of the staff-room met our ears.

"What are you girls doing over there?"

"I told you it was him," Luce whispered with a giggle. "I'll answer."

"No. Let Leah. He knows her."

But Luce was already on her feet and acting outrageously as only Luce can.

"I'm sorry, sir, did you want something?" she called out in a very charming, sophisticated voice.

There was a pause. You could tell he hadn't been expecting such politeness.

"What are you up to down there?" he repeated, toning down the bellow a little.

"Just chatting away, as girls will, sir," Luce offered, cocking her head to one side and raising her shoulders in a very deliberately old-fashioned gesture. To us it was obvious she was taking the mickey, but to anyone who didn't know her, it was quite possible she always spoke in those posh, affected tones and that she was simply being pleasant and polite. Billabong was obviously at a loss which must have made him cross with himself. The staff-room sash window was then pulled down abruptly.

"He's cross now," Leah said. "You should have let me do the talking," she added and the rest of us agreed, but Luce just laughed. Then as soon as the laughter had started it stopped.

"Oh, great!" she announced, sarcastically, as she clutched her bottom. "I've been sitting on a wet bit. I'm soaked."

She turned round, and sure enough there was a large wet patch on the back of her skirt. We couldn't help laughing.

"What am I going to do?" she wailed.

"I dare you to go to the staffroom and ask if any of the teachers has got a hairdrier," I said.

"No, ask Billabong if his technology stretches to thinking of a good way to dry your skirt," Tash suggested, with a wicked grin.

"Yeah, OK," Luce agreed, eyes gleaming. She sauntered off and we all watched her in admiration. We were on the point of turning back round and getting on with our conversation when she came running back.

"It's no good, I can't. I think he really likes me, you see, and I don't want him seeing me like this. I'd rather he saw me at my best – not with a wet bum." Her eyes took on a rapturous look and she clasped her hands together and stared into the middle distance, acting again of course. "One day he'll spot me across a crowded room, his heart will leap and he will know that this is the girl of his dreams…"

"And then he'll wake up and think, 'Thank goodness that nightmare's over!'" Tash finished off, interrupting Luce's soliloquy and sending the rest of us into another giggling fit.

"I'll go," Andy suddenly said. We stopped laughing. "I'll go and get you a hairdrier," she went on. She smiled brightly at us and strolled off.

"Andy's amazing," Jaimini said. "Where does she get her courage from?"

Our gaze followed Andy's small departing figure just as it had followed Luce. But unlike Luce, Andy didn't turn back.

"OK, Jaimini, tell us about yesterday," Tash said, bringing our attention back.

Jaimini explained in detail all the things she had had to do. It sounded as though, out of the four of us who had helped in the café so far, she was easily the most successful. She didn't blow her own trumpet or anything, but Tash and I kept giving each other looks which said, "I'm impressed, how about you?" Then suddenly Jaimini said something which really grabbed my attention.

"This woman – about thirty I guess – was sitting by herself. There was something about her I didn't like when I first set eyes on her, but I couldn't put my finger on what it was. After a bit she called me over and asked for another cappuccino coffee. I went to find Jan to check if I could deal with it myself and Jan said that was fine, so I did. The lady gave me a big smile as I put the cappuccino down and said, 'You *are* doing well, dear. Is this your first day?' and I told her it was, then beat a hasty retreat because she made me feel uncomfortable.

"A few minutes later I saw her talking to Louise. She kept on kind of touching Louise's arm as if stopping her from going. I could tell that Louise was itching to get back to work. She had a tray of dishes in her hands from a table she'd just cleared. Eventually, she managed to get away. As she went past me she said, 'Do me a favour, Jaimini, get that woman at table three a glass of water with four ice cubes in it. Make sure it's exactly four.' She rolled her eyes and added in an undertone, 'Some people!'"

"I took the water over and tried not to plonk it down too much, and I was just going for a quick getaway when she grabbed my arm and pressed something into my hand.

"'Take this, my dear.'

"I opened my hand to find a pound coin.

"'I can't accept any tips, I'm afraid,' I said, as politely as I could, handing it back.

"'Well, that other girl did,' she immediately told me.

"'Yes, but Louise works here properly. I'm just helping today.'

" 'Well, I don't think that's at all fair,' the woman said, raising her voice and attracting a bit of attention. Jan turned round briefly from another table where she was serving.

" 'Oh, yes, it's quite fair,' I said calmly, with what I hoped was a smile. 'As from next week I'll be able to accept tips, and anyway all tips are put in that box over there and we share them out at the end.'

" 'Well, that's where you're wrong,' the woman said, with gleaming spiteful eyes. 'Where's the manageress?'

"I didn't need to call Jan. She was already on her way over.

" 'Can I help you, madam?' she said, leaning forward in the hope that the woman might lower her voice, but there was no chance of that. The woman stood up and pointed an accusing finger at Louise, saying, 'That girl is violating your rules. She took a tip from a couple who have just gone, and put it straight into her pocket. Now I gather from this nice young girl that tips are to be put in that box and shared out. I'm afraid if there's one thing I cannot abide it's dishonesty.'

"Some of the customers were following her speech and enjoying the action, others looked as though they thought her a troublemaker and were deliberately ignoring her and trying to talk loudly amongst themselves. Louise's hand went instinctively into her pocket and she took out two pound coins.

"'See!' said the woman, with a triumphant glance around before her eyes rested on Jan with a now-what-are-you-going-to-do-about-*that*? look.

"'Sorry Jan,' mumbled Louise, going red. 'I got distracted. I was going to put it in that box.'"

Jaimini had us gripped. We all nodded, wide-eyed as if to say, "Yes … go on!"

"Louise went straight over and put it in the box, then escaped into the kitchen. I followed her into the kitchen, too. I'd had enough of that interfering old bag I can tell you." (This was quite a strong statement for Jaimini who tries to see the good in everyone.)

"Anyway," Jaimini went on with her tale, "a

moment later Jan came into the kitchen. She immediately put her arm round Louise, who was nearly in tears, and said, 'Don't you worry, pet.' That's always Jan's affectionate word, isn't it? 'Don't you worry – I know you were going to put that money in the box. That woman's just a troublemaker.'

" 'I don't know why she's got it in for me,' Louise said, a bit shakily.

" 'Neither do I,' Jan answered. 'Perhaps she's jealous because you're better-looking than she is!' Louise managed a smile but she wouldn't go back into the café until the woman had gone."

"What did she look like – this woman?" I asked Jaimini.

"Just ordinary. Brown hair, average, permed. I caught a glimpse of a badge under her coat. I think it said Maggie."

"Maggie?" Tash said, sounding interested. "Now where have I seen that name on a badge before?" She stared into space deep in concentration, then shrugged. "No, can't remember. It'll come back to me."

We forgot about the café then because Andy was strolling calmly back carrying a hairdrier!

"Andy, you're a genius!" cried Luce. "I'm going to the classroom to dry my dress. See you later."

"Where did you get it from?" Leah asked Andy.

"Year ten. One of the girls keeps a hairdrier at school because they like messing about with each other's hair at break times so I decided I'd just go brazenly up to her and ask."

"You've certainly got guts," said Leah. "I'd never dare wander into a year-ten classroom."

"I had to," Andy answered, simply.

"Why?"

"Because once I get an idea in my head, I have to do it, no matter how dangerous or stupid or nerve-racking. I'd disappoint myself so badly if I didn't do it, I just force myself. Anyway, things are nearly always much easier than you think they're going to be," she finished with a smile. I made a mental note to tell Rachel that.

* * *

When I got home from school Rachel was looking out for me. She ran down the road to meet me. "Mum's trying to make me go to Jenny's disco and I can't," she said, looking at me defiantly as though I would instantly take Mum's side. I suddenly had a burst of inspiration.

"Tell you what, let's go to Andy's."

"Why?" she asked, obviously surprised by my apparent change of subject.

"Because…" I hesitated. I wanted to take her to talk to Andy because I had the feeling that Andy would be able to persuade her to go to the disco better than I could.

I ran inside, dumped my school bag, quickly changed, then called out to Mum that Rachel and I were going to Andy's and wouldn't be long.

"Take care on the common," she called back. She always said that. She meant "take care of Rachel". Poor Rachel. Her fear of dogs seemed to be getting worse, not better.

As we wandered on to the common I told Rachel about Andy and the hairdrier, and what she had said about things never turning out to be as bad as you thought they were going to be.

"Well, today was as bad as I thought it was going to be," Rachel replied.

"What happened today?"

She didn't answer straight away because a dog ran past us and she clutched my arm tightly.

"It's OK," I said, prising her fingers off and bending down to stroke the dog. It was an old dog and didn't bark or jump, just wagged its tail gently.

"See, look," I said to Rachel, who stood a safe distance away with rounded shoulders and fists clamped tight in front of her. "He's a lovely soft old thing." The dog licked my ear as though he understood my words. Rachel didn't move or speak. There was a whistle from about fifty metres away and the old fellow ambled off to its owner. Rachel's body uncoiled a little, then gradually relaxed as she told me more about her day. Another emotion took over from her fear – crossness.

"Mrs Gibbs set us a project to do in pairs on any animal of our choice. Well, Jenny and I were going to go together and do guinea pigs. Then it was playtime, and guess whose head appeared over the playground wall? Natalie's."

"Shouldn't she have been at her own school?"

"Yes. She must have been skiving. I'm frightened in case she makes Jenny skive one day, because Jenny always does whatever Natalie tells her to do. Anyway, Jenny went running over to talk to Nattyknickers, and when she came back she didn't want to talk to me any more. She said she was going to do her project with Helen Hayes, all about dogs – so I'm stuck with Kate Bishop. And I'm certain Natalie told Jenny to do dogs on purpose because she knows how scared I am of them. You see what I mean, Fen? Jenny does whatever Natalie tells her to do."

I frowned and thought for a moment, then said, "Anyway, what's wrong with Kate Bishop?"

"Nothing. It's just that nobody really likes her."

"Well, if there's nothing wrong with her, why does nobody like her?"

"I don't know … she's a bit weird, that's all. She's on her own a lot and she's got red hair and freckles…"

"Hold on a sec… One of my best friends has got reddish hair and freckles … and she's a bit weird, but there's nothing wrong with that. You mustn't follow the crowd so much, Rachel. Why not invite Kate to tea and do some of your project together?"

All the time I was saying all this I was feeling very hypocritical because I knew how easy it was to follow the crowd. There was a girl called Lizzie in our year at school and I'd never dream of being chatty and friendly with her. And why not? Simply because I'd heard she wasn't very nice, and like everybody else I couldn't be bothered to find out for myself.

"Look!" cried Rachel, out of the blue. She was clutching my arm which made me think, uh-oh more dogs!

"Over there! It's them!" she whispered, urgently.

"Who?" I whispered back, even though we were miles from anyone's earshot.

"Jenny and Natalie... Look – in that tree. I'm certain it's them. I recognize that curly pony-tail and those thin legs."

"Good, let's go and say hello," I said, feeling quite glad to have the chance at last to see the object of my sister's hate.

"No fear," Rachel said, tugging my arm. "Let's go back home. *Please*, Fen."

"No. Come on. She won't be horrible with me here."

"Well, you can go and see them if you want but I'm going home."

She walked a few steps then turned back to me. "Oh, please come too, Fen."

I felt really sad for her at that moment because she'd suddenly realized that she couldn't go back home without me in case any dogs came bounding up to meet her.

"OK, we'll compromise," I said. "We'll go past them, but not too close and we'll just call out 'Hi'. OK?"

"OK," she said.

As we drew nearer and nearer to Natalie and Jenny, Rachel kept up a whispered running commentary on various nasty things that the American girl had done. The more I heard, the more I began to wonder a little uncomfortably whether Rachel wasn't becoming a touch over-imaginative. I'd never met Natalie of course, but Jenny I knew quite well. Some of Rachel's tales involving Jenny made it sound as though she was a real monster and not the sweet little Jenny who's been hanging out with my sister for so long. The running commentary stopped the moment we got within earshot.

The girls were experimenting hanging by their legs from a long strong branch. They were giggling a lot and not getting very far. I was certain they hadn't seen us. Jenny was actually upside down when she spotted us.

She swung up to a sitting position and said, "Hi, Fen. Hi, Rachel." Then she looked at Natalie, and I felt Rachel tense beside me.

"Hi," I called back. Rachel didn't say anything. Natalie had had her back towards us. As she turned to face us I saw how very pretty she was. Her hair was falling out of its pony-tail and hanging in wispy, blonde strands around her face and she had dirty bark stains on her white jeans, but despite that she looked lovely standing on that branch with her hands stretched up to the one above. Her face broke into a big smile. I tried to dislike her but at that moment I couldn't. If she was faking that warm friendly smile she deserved an Oscar.

"Uh-oh," she said jumping down from the tree. "Go on! Shoo! Off you go!"

Rachel was clutching me again and I could feel her trembling. A large retriever was pant-ing and jumping about excitedly beside her. Natalie got hold of the dog's collar and pulled him away, saying, "Come on. What's your name, huh?" She looked at the identity chain on the collar, and picking up a gnarled little chunk of bark, she hurled it into the distance and called out, "Go fetch, Rumbelow!"

Rumbelow needed no second asking. He

barked happily at Natalie as if to say, "Thanks, I was just hoping someone might take the initiative and throw me something to fetch." Then he leapt into the air and ran full pelt towards the bark. We heard a whistle from somewhere. Rumbelow heard it too because he loped away from the bark and off to the other side of the common to rejoin his owner.

"It's OK now," I said to Rachel, removing her clutching fingers from my arm, as Natalie came and put a protective arm round her shoulders. I watched in amazement. She seemed so nice. Rachel's eyes met mine with a message. I couldn't read the message except that it was something very important she wanted to say but couldn't.

"Can Rachel stay and play with us for a while?" Natalie asked. "We'll shoo the dogs away," she added, with a grin.

I grinned back. She was impossible to dislike. Her American accent was really strong. I'd never heard an accent quite like it on television or anything.

"No!" Rachel said abruptly and rather

loudly. She must have realized how silly that had sounded.

"No … I mean … I can't…" she stumbled, "because we've got to see Andy, haven't we, Fen?"

Her eyes were really boring into mine now. They were pleading with me to take her away from these monsters, yet all I could see were two very kind, friendly girls. I couldn't help feeling that it would do her good to stay and play for a while. She'd obviously got the whole Jenny/Natalie thing out of proportion.

"Tell you what, I'll pop over to Andy's myself. I'll only be a little while then I'll come back and collect you. What about that?"

"But I wanted to see Andy's little brother…" Rachel insisted.

"No, stay with us," Natalie encouraged her. "We've got a great game of Tree Home going, and we sure need someone to be the mom."

I didn't know what on earth she was talking about, but it sounded like the kind of thing Rachel liked playing. I thought I saw Natalie nudge Jenny.

"Yeah, stay Rachel, go on," Jenny said, but somehow she didn't sound quite so enthusiastic as Natalie.

"I'll be back in less than half an hour," I told Rachel, giving her an encouraging but firm smile, and absolutely no chance to argue without looking very foolish.

"OK," she whispered, reminding me for a second of a balloon with all the air gone out of it.

I glanced back a couple of times as I crossed to the other side of the common. I could hear Natalie's laughter. I couldn't hear Rachel or Jenny at all, but they all looked to be playing together all right.

For the short distance to Andy's I thought about Rachel's behaviour. Why was she so loath to be with Jenny and Natalie especially when Natalie had been so thoughtful and kind about the dog? I was puzzled. Then I started to feel worried. Oh dear, what if poor Rachel was having a tough time. What if Natalie and Jenny had pulled the wool over my eyes and put on that nice friendly act purely for my benefit? No. Impossible. I dismissed the thought out of hand because no two nine-year-olds could fake an act like that.

Before I knew it I was standing outside Andy's front door. I had been so wrapped up in my thoughts I hadn't noticed anything on my short journey since the tree on the common. I knocked on the door and at the very moment of knocking I realized something. Of course! Andy wouldn't be there. How stupid of me to forget. It was Friday, her trial day at the café.

Andy's mum, Dominique, answered the door. Her face had an anxious look. When she saw that it was me, the look turned to one that I can only describe as panic. Her eyes strayed behind me and I turned round, following her gaze. I had been so deep in thought about Rachel that I hadn't noticed the dark green car that occupied the drive. There shouldn't be anything odd about a car in a drive, of course, except that this one had a French registration plate.

Oh, no, I thought, as I turned back and met Dominique's eyes.

"My husband ees back unexpectedly from France," she said, in a small voice.

Chapter 7

A tall dark man with sallow skin and slightly slanting, rather hooded eyes appeared behind Dominique. His voice when he spoke was heavy with sarcasm.

"Unless Agnès has undergone an amazing transformation, this is not she."

His eyes were addressing Dominique, and yet I felt he should be looking at me as he was talking about me and I was the visitor. I took an instant dislike to him.

Dominique was trying to pull herself together. I was just standing there feeling horribly worried and also very guilty because

Andy's dad's eyes had begun to scrutinize my face.

"You wouldn't have any idea where Andy ees?" Dominique asked me in a steady voice which gave no clue that her eyes were flashing the message "For goodness sake, don't mention the café."

I thought fast. If I said she was with one of her friends he'd get on the phone and they unknowingly might let the cat out of the bag. If I said I didn't know where she was, he could easily flip and start contacting the police and sending out search parties.

I suddenly felt terribly responsible. After all, it was my pressure on Mum and Mum's pressure on Dominique which persuaded her to allow Andy to do the café job. If only Mum was with me, she'd know what to do. I tried to think what exactly Mum *would* do. She'd probably tell Mr Sorrell the truth. "Mr Sorrell, your daughter is actually helping out at the café." Not working – just helping. Yes, that was it! I'd tell the truth, because she was only helping after all.

No, no! I couldn't tell the truth. It was obvious that if she was helping there was something fishy going on. Mr Sorrell had expressly forbidden Andy to work at the café, so he wouldn't take kindly to what could only possibly be a trial run.

All these thoughts had come and gone in just a couple of seconds, yet my head felt as though a tornado had taken up residence in it. Then quite out of the blue the tornado suddenly whipped and whistled away leaving nothing but calm.

"Andy's got athletics practice at school," I said, with what I hoped was a relaxed smile at Mr Sorrell. Nothing resembling a relaxed smile was returned by him, though. His eyes narrowed and he bent forward a little as if he were grilling me for information on the enemy. "Athletics practice?" he said slowly, as though I had just dropped into the conversation that Andy had left home to join a religious commune or something.

"Yes, I think there's a meeting in a couple of weeks… It's an extra practice." I stopped there, even though it was tempting to add a little bit more information … and then a little bit more.

If ever you're in the situation of having to tell a white lie because you have no choice, remember to make it short and to the point. The more frills you add, the less convincing you sound. The same applies to making excuses for not being able to go somewhere. Just give one excuse, not four. I learnt that a year or so ago.

"And at what time does the athletics meeting conclude?" Mr Sorrell asked with raised eyebrows and his head tilted. The sarcasm hadn't left his voice and I was still under scrutiny. Why couldn't he just say, "What time does the meeting end?" like anyone else would? I can't stand people who use words like *conclude* when they could just say *end*. And while we're on the subject, why couldn't he have the good manners to ask my name?

"Six o'clock," I told him.

"Six o'clock? That's a late finish for an unscheduled after school event."

"It *was* scheduled!" I blurted out. "That's what I came to tell Dominique. You see, Andy forgot to mention about the meeting so she asked me to pop over and tell you."

"Don't they have telephones at the school?" (Another dose of his hateful sarcasm.)

"Andy knew I was coming this way with my sister, so I offered to pop in." I managed a weak smile at Dominique. She smiled back encouragingly, though she still looked worried.

"Poppin, Poppin!" came a squeaky voice, imitating my own last words. The owner of the voice followed. What a lovely relief it was to see Sebastien looking just as he had looked the other day – nappy round his thighs, bib round his back. Mr Sorrell swung him up and held him. "Well, in that case," he said, as though he were calling an end to the conversation, "I shall go and pick her up at six o'clock. That will surprise her."

He smiled, but it didn't quite reach his eyes. Poor Andy. If I were her, I'd love it when he went to France and I'd dread his ever coming home. Sebastien was wriggling and whining. He wanted to get down. Who wouldn't? Mr Sorrell lowered him awkwardly to the ground and brushed his hands off as though he'd been doing a bit of weeding.

I glanced at my watch. Four-thirty. That gave me an hour and a half to do something. I wasn't quite sure what exactly.

"I'd better go," I said.

Dominique gave me a sort of imploring look. I wished Andy's dad would disappear, then I could reassure her that I would deliver Andy safely home before her father even set out to collect her. Fortunately he turned and strolled back into the house at that moment.

"I'll go and get her back, don't worry," I whispered to Dominique. She nodded and patted my shoulder.

"Bye, Fen," she said. "Thanks for letting us know about the meeting."

Mr Sorrell reappeared.

"So this is Fen," he said, weightily. "Why didn't you say so?" he asked me.

"Because you didn't ask," I retorted rather rudely. I was past caring what impression I created, though I didn't like the way his eyes narrowed when I said that. He suddenly broke into a grin as though my words had pressed a button that changed his mood.

"Well, Fen, it's such a lovely day, I think I'll join you and stroll over the common, then watch the athletics." He emphasized the word *athletics* as though it were in some way significant, but I couldn't work out the significance, and another tornado was crashing heavily in my direction. I had to stop Mr Sorrell. Help! I couldn't stop him.

Yes, I could! I could say that the athletics meeting was taking place at another venue and that Andy had gone on a minibus. No, that would anger him. He'd want to know why the school allowed its pupils to go off somewhere without first asking parents' permission. Then he'd probably conduct a full scale investigation into the seat-belt situation. No, I had to get to that café as fast as I could and get Andy back to school double quick.

"May I use the phone, please?" I asked, politely. "Mum asked me to get something from the shop on my way and I can't for the life of me remember what it was."

"Yes, of course, Fen," Dominique answered, quickly. "It's in the kitchen."

I could hear her talking to her husband as I went into the kitchen.

"Why don't you take Sebastien, darling? He would love to get out in the fresh air. I'll get the buggy."

I didn't hear the answer. I tapped in Tash's number and prayed that Peta wouldn't be anywhere near the phone. It rang eleven times. With each ring my heart felt a little heavier. I put it down on the eleventh. There was nothing for it. I'd just have to phone the café and tell Andy to get over to school as fast as she could. The question was, should I tell the truth or not, because it was sure to be Jan who answered the phone? I stared at Dominique's phone while I thought about this. The dreaded voice cut into my thoughts. I looked up. He was leaning against the kitchen doorway. "Not forgotten your own number, surely?" he said with his usual sarcasm.

"No, there was no reply. I was just wondering where Mum might be… If you want to set off, Mr Sorrell, I'll be along in a sec…"

"No hurry, take your time," he answered, with a smile. There was a bit of a challenge in that slightly mocking smile and it crossed my mind that he might have known all along where Andy was. He was still standing there. I had to phone the café though, so I did.

As I tapped in the last number I heard Dominique's voice calling from the hall. "Sebastien's all ready, darling," then in quite another tone. "Go on leetle *cornichon*, go see Papa."

Yes, come on, little gherkin, I thought, come and smear some nice soft sticky rusk all over Daddy's trousers so he'll have to go and change them. My imaginings became wilder as I listened to the phone ringing in the café… And then be sick all over Daddy's shirt so he's got to change that as well… In fact, little gherkin, if you went one stage further and weed all over Daddy's shoes, he might even change his mind and not go out at all.

"Good afternoon. *The Café*. May I help you?" came Jan's politest manageress's voice. I looked up. Mr Sorrell had gone.

I held the mouthpiece as close to my mouth as possible and spoke in an undertone.

"It's me, Jan. I'm really sorry about this, but I'm phoning from Andy's place. An emergency has cropped up and she's got to come home."

There was a brief silence. Jan's voice sounded fairly neutral when she spoke next – not warm, not cold. "I'll fetch Andy and you can have a quick word."

"Thanks, Jan."

Andy came on the phone sounding surprised.

"Hi, Fen, what's happened?"

I had my back to the door but something made me turn round. Mr Sorrell was peering into the pantry door with his back to me. My heart thudded horribly. There was only one thing for it. "Just a moment…" I said into the mouthpiece, then deliberately not covering it,

I said, "I shan't be a sec, Mr Sorrell. You go ahead and I'll catch up. You know how to get to the school, don't you? You keep to your left right across the common and you'll see the stile at the other end. It's left of the play area."

"Yes, I know," came Andy's dad's voice. I hoped fervently that Andy could hear it. There was more I had to get over to her. "Andy'll most likely come out of the second entrance from school – you know the place where there's the gap in the hedge?"

"You'll be telling me how I'll recognize my own daughter next. Will she be wearing a pink carnation and carrying a copy of the *Telegraph*, Fen?"

He smirked at his own wit. I managed an odd little laugh. There was still one thing I had to let Andy know.

"Oh, what am I talking about? Of course she won't be coming out of the second entrance, unless the athletics meeting finishes before six of course, but I'm pretty sure she said six o'clock."

He gave me a sharp little nod, which I suppose was his own charming little way of saying thank you for the information.

I spoke into the mouthpiece. "Sorry about that, Mum."

"*Mum!*" Andy's voice squealed at about a thousand decibels. I pressed the phone more tightly to my ear and prayed that Mr Sorrell hadn't recognized his daughter's voice. A quick glance at his narrowed eyes made my heart start its dangerous thudding again. "Oh, Emmy," I said, "it's you. I thought Mum was still on the phone."

"Is he standing there or something?" Andy whispered, sounding petrified.

"Yes, that's right, baked beans," I managed with a slight tremor in my voice.

"What shall I say to Jan?" Andy asked urgently.

My brain went into overdrive and I managed to come up with something.

"Not another migraine," I said as though I was humouring a young child. "You look after the rest of the family," I added in motherly tones. "I've got to go now but I'll be back in a few minutes. Bye."

Without waiting for Andy's reply I put the phone down and turned to Mr Sorrell. "My little sister is playing Doctors with her dolls," I told him with an indulgent smile, then I strode past him and also past a pale-faced Dominique who was gently rocking backwards and forwards a plush little buggy containing Sebastien, who was fast asleep.

I now needed to slow this whole thing down so that Andy would have time to get changed and set off home from the direction of the school.

I prayed that she had got the message, and would greet her dad with a breezy, "Hi, Dad, what a lovely surprise – and guess what, the athletics meeting finished early." A horrible thought burst in. There wouldn't be athletics in the autumn term would there? Oh, what a stupid mistake to make! That might explain Mr Sorrell's cynical look. Well, Andy would just have to say that I got it wrong and it was netball practice.

"Why don't you come too, Dominique?" I said to Andy's mum, with a bright smile followed by a significant glance at her tight smart skirt and high heels. She got the message.

"Oh, that's a good idea. I'll just get changed," she said, running lightly upstairs.

At that point I remembered Rachel. I clapped a hand over my mouth. "Sorry, I've got to go. My sister's waiting for me – I just remembered…"

Mr Sorrell was looking at me as though I was mad.

"Sorry. Bye."

With that I ran out of the drive and all the way to the common thinking, now it's up to Andy. I've done all I can. I began to scan the common for the three girls.

I was rapidly approaching the tree where I had left them and yet there was not a sign of any girls on it or anywhere near it. Perhaps they'd gone to Jenny's house. Oh dear, that was probably exactly what Rachel was dreading happening. I began to imagine the scenario.

JENNY: *Come on, I'm bored. Let's go back to my place.*

RACHEL: *I'll just stay here because Fen'll wonder where I am otherwise.*

NATALIE: *Gee, in America we don't have this crazy thing about big sisters watching over liddle sisters.*

JENNY: *Yeah, come on Rachel, don't act like such a baby.*

RACHEL: *What about the…*

NATALIE: *Oh, I get it. She's scared of your dog, Jenny. This kid is so sad.*

JENNY: *Ignore the dog, Rachel.*

RACHEL: *I can't…*

JENNY: (YANKING RACHEL TO HER FEET) *Yes, you can.* (JENNY AND NATALIE FROGMARCH A MISERABLE RACHEL ALONG TO JENNY'S HOUSE.)

I suddenly felt like the cruellest, most insensitive sister in the world. I shook my head to try to get rid of my horrible imaginings. I kept trying to tell myself that they were having a great time at Jenny's. Right. So what should I do? Why was life so complicated? Is this how top secret agents felt – continually planning and precision-timing their next move in order to combat the enemy? There were three enemies in my life at the moment. Well – one definite and two possibles. Mr Sorrell, and Natalie and Jenny. I decided to go home and see if Rachel was there. If she wasn't I would phone Jenny's and if necessary, Natalie's.

I kept up a steady jog all the way home and tried to concentrate on how much good it was doing me.

"Hello, you look exhausted!" was Mum's smiling greeting. "I think I'll come with you next time you decide to go for a run... Where's Rachel?"

That answered my first question. "I think she's at Jenny's. I'll phone."

"What do you mean, you think? Why didn't you keep her with you? You didn't leave her on the common, I hope?"

"Not on her own. It's OK. Jenny and Natalie were there."

"But Rachel can't stand Jenny and Natalie at the moment."

"Yes I know, but she … she wanted to stay…"

No, she didn't, I thought. Oh, how utterly stupid I'd been. I must have looked really distraught because Mum's voice and face softened.

"I'm sure you had her best interests at heart."

"Yes … yes I did," I said. "You see, they were being so nice to Rachel. Natalie even put her arm round her when a dog came bounding up. So when they asked Rachel to stay with them for a little while – just while I went to Andy's – I thought it would be good for Rachel. They never said they were going anywhere. I said I'd be back in half an hour and I guess it was about that."

"I'll phone Jenny's mum," Mum said, looking tight-lipped, but more with the situation than with me.

"Hello, Ruth, it's Dee Brooks. You haven't by any chance got Rachel at your place have you…? Oh, good… That's nice… No, I'll send Fen along to collect her right away, thanks all the same… Yes… OK. Thanks for having her, Ruth… Bye."

Mum turned to me. "They're playing in the garden, apparently. Everything seems to be perfectly all right, but I'm not happy about her going off like that."

"I'll go and fetch her," I said, opening the door.

As I walked to Jenny's I wondered how Andy was getting on. Hopefully she would be safely approaching the common, kit bag over her shoulder, about to have a joyous reunion with her nasty father. Perhaps Andy didn't find him nasty. It was funny, this family thing. It's strange how we all instinctively love our parents. Even though we hate their guts at times – underneath we love them. I made a mental note to ask Tash what she thought about my dad. I mean, maybe she found him just as nasty as I found Andy's dad. You can't really judge your own parents very well.

I knocked at Jenny's front door and waited. There was no reply. I was about to ring the bell when I decided to go round to the back.

That way I could see the girls before they saw me, which meant I could judge the atmosphere properly and see how they were getting on.

I walked without a sound round the side of the house and gently pushed open the gate at the back. The first thing I heard was their German shepherd dog barking. Then I heard giggling. The sight that met my eyes made my blood run cold.

Natalie was standing near the back door with a ball in her hand. She threw the ball hard, saying, "Go on, Digby, go fetch." The ball and the dog were hurtling towards a large oak tree at the bottom of the long garden. Jenny sat on a garden table with her feet on the bench and clapped. Up in the oak, clinging to a branch and looking deathly pale and terrified, was Rachel. I took in the situation at a glance. They were deliberately taunting my sister with their cruel game. None of them had noticed me standing there.

"Here, Jenny, your turn," Natalie said, handing the ball to Jenny. "Send it harder than I did. I like watching her face when Digby crashes into the tree." Natalie clasped her hands together in gleeful anticipation, and I thought I was going to be sick. A look of worry flickered across Jenny's face, but she went, nevertheless, to the back door with the ball.

"Stop it!" I yelled at the top of my voice. "Stop your nasty wicked game this minute!"

Jenny stood stock still and stared at me wide-eyed and fearful. Natalie on the other hand, bent down and started stroking the dog. She looked up at me defiantly from her squatting position as if to say, "You don't worry me with your big voice."

I ignored her and went over to the tree. "It's all right, Rachel. I'll have you away from these hateful girls in a minute. I never should have left you in the first place." Then I yanked the dog by its collar, away from the surprised-looking Natalie, who nearly fell over. What a pity she didn't.

Without saying a word I led the dog past the gawping Jenny, up the steps, and without even knocking I pushed open the back door, thrust him inside, shut the back door, brushed my hands together dismissively and went back to Rachel. Her face was still white and she was trembling as I helped her down from the tree. Nobody spoke as I guided her across the lawn towards the gate.

We were on the point of going out through the gate, when Natalie's voice, calm and cool, rang out over the garden, "Gee, Jenny, your mom isn't going to be too pleased."

"No, she isn't," I snapped back in my harshest tones, "especially when I tell her how her daughter is being corrupted by an evil American girl."

At that she had the nerve to smirk. "I meant, she won't be too pleased with you for putting the dirty dog indoors without wiping his feet, or checking that the kitchen door through to the rest of the house was closed."

She strolled over and linked her arm through Jenny's. "Come on, Jenny, let's go pick your mom some flowers." Jenny looked pale and shocked but she allowed herself to be led away to pick flowers – another subtle little move on Natalie's part.

"Come on, Rachel," I said, "let's get out of here." But the back door opened and Mrs Cranston stormed into the garden.

"Who put Digby inside just now?" she demanded with her arms folded and her head on one side. "Because he's padded all over the house with his dirty feet."

"She did," Natalie said, pointing at me.

Mrs Cranston's eyes travelled round to where I was standing. She was torn between two emotions. She was trying to be cross, yet she couldn't help breaking off for a second to say, "Hello, Fen. How are you?"

"Hello, Mrs Cranston, I'm sorry about the dog … you see…"

Her crossness came back.

"So it *was* you who put him in the kitchen with his dirty feet. I can't believe it of you, Fen…"

"I had a very good reason," I began, but obviously I chose the wrong words because Mrs Cranston suddenly went berserk.

"You don't come round here and take it upon yourself to decide where my dog should go, Fen! I don't care how good the reason is. And now you're just disappearing without so much as a goodbye, are you? I shall have to have a word with your mother, young lady."

She turned to the others.

"You two had better come in for tea… Oh … Natalie, aren't they lovely. That's very sweet of you, dear."

Natalie had been steadily picking flowers during Mrs Cranston's attack on me, and she had presented the little bouquet with an appropriately coy smile, just as Mrs Cranston was running out of steam.

"'Oh, Natalie, aren't they lovely,'" I mimicked Mrs Cranston in a stupid voice. I couldn't help it. It just came out. I'd had enough of Natalie getting away with everything. I didn't care how rude I was to anyone any more. I had completely lost my temper.

"Natalie is lethal, Mrs Cranston, and if only you'd ask a few questions and get to the bottom of things, instead of standing there and giving me grief about your stupid great hound dirtying your pristine house, then maybe you'd learn the truth about that evil American girl, and also about the terrible influence she's having on your own daughter, whose behaviour this afternoon in helping to paralyse my sister with fear is totally unforgivable. Grounding her for a whole month wouldn't be enough of a punishment for Jenny, and as for that American pain in the bum over there, she needs to go back where she came from, preferably by rowing boat, and preferably alone!"

My voice had risen to a shrill shriek at the end of my speech. My heart was beating wildly. I felt high as a kite. My body shook and my eyes flashed as my emotions surged. I shall always remember that moment because everyone around me was stunned and speechless, and it was I who had achieved that.

I took Rachel's hand and led her through the gate, not bothering to shut it behind me. My knees wobbled for at least fifty metres.

"That was amazing, Fen!" Rachel said finally.

I couldn't decide from that whether she meant amazingly wonderful or amazingly awful.

"Amazingly what?" I asked, tentatively.

"Amazingly amazing!" she breathed.

Chapter 8

During the rest of the journey home Rachel told me what had been happening since I'd left her on the common.

Natalie had almost immediately proposed going back to Jenny's. Jenny had been reluctant and made up a few excuses. Rachel had insisted she should stay and wait for Fen. Natalie had then pointed out that if she stayed all alone and a dog came along, she'd be terrified. Rachel had been forced to agree and had therefore gone back to Jenny's house with the feeling that she was being led into the lion's den.

"It was OK at first," she told me softly, "because we played at secretaries in Jenny's bedroom. But then Natalie said she was bored and wanted to go outside. I asked Jenny quietly where the dog was and she said, 'It's all right, he's in the utility room.'

"That's a little room that leads off the kitchen," Rachel explained to me. "It's especially for Digby. I noticed the door from the utility room to the kitchen was shut, when we went out of the back door into the garden. Then after a bit Natalie said she was going to the Jim – that's what Americans call the loo – and when she·came back out again, she left the back door open."

"She was going to the *what*?" I asked.

"To the Jim," repeated Rachel. "That's what Americans call the loo."

"It's the john, not the Jim," I told Rachel.

"She definitely said the Jim."

"Presumably that's her idea of a joke. Anyway, what happened next?"

"About thirty seconds later, out bounded Digby, barking and excited. I just knew from the satisfied look on Natalie's face that she'd opened the utility-room door and deliberately left the back door open, so he'd hear our voices and come outside. I also bet it was she who left the door from the kitchen through to the rest of the house open, so she could blame that on someone else, too.

"I ran to the tree and climbed up because it was the only place where Digby couldn't get near me. He immediately tried, of course. He hurtled after me and started leaping and barking up at me. I was only just out of his reach because I couldn't get any higher up in the tree. He reminded me of the wolf in *Peter and the Wolf*, and I was the cat. I'll never, ever listen to that cassette again.

"Natalie found it hysterically funny. Jenny didn't laugh at first, and neither did she want to play Natalie's game, but — I don't know what it is about Natalie — you have to do what she says because she'll make things ten times worse if you don't."

Poor Rachel. How I hated myself for having left her. "You poor thing," I said giving her a quick hug. "I'm sorry I left you on the common. It just seemed such a good opportunity for you to get back in with Jenny. I never realized what a monster that Natalie is."

"Wherever have you two been?" was Mum's greeting as we walked in.

"It's a long story," I told Mum.

"Yes, it must be," Mum said, "judging from the phone call I had earlier."

I sat down heavily. Mrs Cranston had obviously wasted no time at all. It looked as though I was in for another hard time.

"So who phoned?" I asked Mum in a tired voice.

She obviously didn't like my tone because her answer was delivered snappily. "Jan, of course."

"Jan!"

Mum had taken me quite by surprise because I had forgotten all about Andy.

"Yes, she was wondering if you'd like to pop over and finish Andy's stint at the café, as it was you who called the café to alert Andy that she was urgently needed to look after her mother, who was suffering near collapse with a migraine, and there was nobody to look after Sebastien. I couldn't understand why you'd said you were going to see Andy when you knew perfectly well she was at the café..."

"I just forgot, that's all."

"The whole thing strikes me as rather suspicious, because when I phoned Dominique to see if I could be of any help, her husband answered!"

"Oh, no! What exactly did you say to Mr Sorrell, Mum? You didn't mention the café, did you?"

"No, I've got more sense than that. I just asked to speak to Dominique. She came on the phone, and when I asked her if she was OK, she said, 'Actually we were just going to stroll across the common and meet Andy from school, but thanks all the same.'"

"Well, that's it, Mum. Don't you see? Mr Sorrell has arrived home unexpectedly. Dominique is petrified that he's going to hit the roof if he finds out about Andy and the café, so I phoned the café and alerted Andy. I told Mr Sorrell that she was at an athletics practice at school."

"Oh dear," Mum said, also sitting down heavily. "I don't like to think that I may be partly responsible for Andy and her mum having to deceive her dad. I hadn't realized how afraid Dominique is of her husband. I thought she was just being cautious in not telling him, and of course, all the time he's in France there's not really a problem, but if he's going to keep popping home, that's quite different."

"I think he's only at home for this weekend."

Emmy had been painting at the kitchen table with her tongue sticking out of her mouth during all this.

"Right, I think we've had enough of that conversation," she suddenly announced. "I'm starving."

Mum, Rachel and I all managed a faint sigh of a laugh. On Friday evenings we all eat together when Dad gets home, so Emmy is always hungry and whiny for about an hour beforehand, because it's later than her usual teatime.

"I'll start making it right now!" Mum said,

jumping up and heading towards the vegetable rack. At that point the phone rang.

"I'll get it," I said. "Hello."

"I'd like to speak to your mother please, Fen. It's Mrs Cranston."

My heart sank and a million excuses entered my head but never quite reached my voice box. "Mum's not here." "Mum's ill." "Mum's out." Of course I couldn't say any of them with Mum standing in the same room, so I just handed her the phone while covering the mouthpiece, and tried to give a potted self-defence in three seconds.

"It's Mrs Cranston, Mum, and whatever she says I triple promise you that she's got it wrong. I was only rude to her because of poor Rachel."

Then I said to Rachel and Emmy, "Come on, you two, let's go and play Cluedo in my room." So we trooped upstairs, the weary one, the silent one and the whiny one. It was less than two minutes before we heard Dad's car door slam and then his key turn in the door.

"Daddy!" shrieked Emmy, jumping up.

"Just give him a minute to get through the door and say hello to Mum," I told her. Luckily, she was pretty absorbed in the Cluedo otherwise she would have ignored me and gone belting off, but I managed to hold her back for a couple of minutes, then she went off whoosh like a rocket and Rachel and I followed behind her slowly.

"Here we go again," I thought, though at least this time I'd have Rachel to verify my story, and the only thing I'd actually done wrong was leaving Rachel on the common. I suppose there was also the small matter of my telling Mrs Cranston, in no uncertain terms, exactly where I thought she should get off. Oh, yes, then there was the other tiny detail of criticizing her daughter and her daughter's guest. Every time I thought about Natalie my fists clenched in anger.

As Rachel and I went into the kitchen Emmy was just crashing into Dad's knees and hugging them tightly while chanting loudly, "Another weekend is here. Hooray." Dad heaved her up and she reached out for Mum to join in the hug. So with one arm round each of their necks she pulled everybody's faces in together and said, "Come on. Let's all say it…" Then she yelled out at the top of her voice, "Another weekend is here. Hooray!" Mum and Dad groaned and tried in vain to cover their ears. Emmy was beginning to go over the top. "Now, Rachel and Fenny join in, come on…"

Dad glanced over and must have detected our less than joyous mood because he unpeeled Emmy from his neck and came over to where Rachel and I sat at the table. He put an arm round each of us. He was definitely in frivolous mode because he said, "Well, Dee, you've managed to pick up a couple of good staff here. I particularly like this one with the long hair and the radiantly happy smile." (He's a past master at sarcasm is our dad.)

I stuck my tongue out jokingly and said, "You won't particularly like this one with the long hair and the radiantly happy smile when you hear the latest crime she's committed."

"Uh-oh!" said Dad, in a silly squeaky voice, obviously determined that nothing was going to spoil his weekend cheer. "Well, in that case I shall have to turn my attention to the long-legged pale beauty on my right!" Rachel smiled weakly, then she giggled loudly and squirmed about because Dad had started tickling her ribs, a favourite ploy of his for getting any of us laughing when we're sulky.

Mum was concentrating on her cooking. She only just managed to smile at Dad's antics. I wondered when she planned to confront me with my misdemeanours. I didn't have to wonder for long.

"Fen, I'll come straight to the point. I've heard what Mrs Cranston has to say. Now I'd like to hear your side of the story."

At this point Rachel surprised me. "No, Mum, I want you to hear *my* side of the story."

Mum looked taken aback but nodded as if her vocal cords weren't up to making any contribution at that moment. Dad just looked utterly baffled. So Rachel began.

I watched Mum and Dad and Emmy

throughout Rachel's soliloquy. They were all totally still. Emmy's eyes grew wide with horror when Rachel described the dog game. Mum had tears in her eyes and Dad looked furious.

When Rachel talked about my entry on the scene, she made me out to be a quick-thinking, compassionate, strong-minded heroine. It was absolutely brilliant. Emmy broke out of her intense wide-eyed gaze for a few seconds to plant a massive wet kiss on my cheek, and to announce, "Fen, you're the best big sister in the entire world, in fact in the whole universe, in fact in inFITiny!"

"InFINity," I corrected.

"Yes, InFITiny."

"That's enough, Emmy," said Dad. "Go on, Rachel."

I was dying to hear how I was going to remain the heroine while delivering an extremely rude speech to Rachel's best friend's mum. Emmy sat down again and resumed her staring act as if she'd been obliged to break off for a few moments during her favourite TV programme.

"Well," said Rachel. She drew in a deep breath, then let it out again as though she'd lost her thread. We all looked at her. She drew another breath and began to tell what I'd said to Mrs Cranston, but she couldn't remember properly and her voice wavered because she was obviously torn between trying to stick to the truth and not getting me into too deep trouble. I decided to take over at this point. I looked at Dad. I knew he was as angry as I had been about the dog game so I tried to rekindle that anger in him before telling him about the awful speech.

"Imagine how it was for me, Dad. I'd opened the back gate, not knowing what I was going to find. I saw the venomous expression on that American girl's face and realized how she'd tried to get Jenny under her spell. The worst bit was when she said to Jenny, 'Send the ball harder than I did, I like watching her face when Digby crashes into the tree.' And you should have seen little Rachel, Dad, she was eaten up with fear. Well, you can see how I must have felt."

Dad nodded grimly two or three times. He was just as angry as I had been.

"I had to get her out of that situation as fast as I could but I also wanted to throttle Jenny and kill Natalie." I paused here for dramatic effect. Dad just nodded again. "I would have managed to leave the premises without doing either of those things if Mrs Cranston hadn't appeared and started going mad because of a few dirty paw prints over her ridiculously clean house. I could feel my patience being severely tried.

"Then when Natalie gave her the flowers, and Mrs Cranston understood from the fact that I said, 'Sorry about the dog', that it had been *me* who had opened the door to the rest of the house, and she started ranting at me, well... I just snapped.

"I basically told her she should get her facts straight before laying into me, and all I'd done was rescue my sister from her own daughter and her hateful American friend who ought to get back to America, preferably in a rowing boat on her own."

I had stated my case. I now hung my head and waited for the thunderstorm.

Instead, there was a great roar of laughter from Dad. He stood up, came round to my side of the table, heaved me to my feet, slapped me on the back, gave me a big hug followed by another slap on the back, and said, "Bravo, Fen. Bravo! I couldn't have put it better myself. I wish I'd been there to see the look on the old bag's face. It's always got on my nerves, that squeaky clean house of hers, and you were quite right, she should have got her facts right."

"Um, excuse me, Trevor," came Mum's brittle-sounding voice, breaking into my euphoria, "but aren't you forgetting something?"

Dad and I looked at Mum. I clung to Dad. He had absolutely seen my point of view and I was grateful.

"What are we forgetting?" he asked, sounding rather irritated.

"The fact that Fen was extremely rude to one of our friends, who, let's face it, was not acquainted with the facts, and should *never* have been on the receiving end of Fen's temper."

Dad released his bear-hug hold on me and a little of the joy I had felt at his reaction began to wither. I began a silent prayer – "Please, don't let Dad be talked out of his own feelings."

Again Rachel flew to my rescue.

"Mum, all I can say is that if you'd seen what Fen saw, I bet you would have reacted in the same way."

Mum's eyelids fluttered – always a sign that she's unsure of herself, but no, she was coming right back, and Dad had let go of me altogether now.

"Trevor, you didn't hear Mrs Cranston just now on the phone. She was absolutely furious. She agreed that Fen was right, that she didn't know her facts, but that that was absolutely no excuse for Fen to talk like that."

"Well, I agree with Rachel and Fen and Daddy," Emmy piped up enthusiastically, but not very helpfully because it made Dad make his position clear, and from the sounds of it he wasn't quite so firmly in my camp as he had seemed to be at first.

"Hold on a minute. This isn't school, Emmy. We're not taking sides. I'd like to talk with your mum on her own. Off you go, you lot – what about a quick burst of Cluedo, hmm?"

We trooped off for the second time that day, Emmy grabbing a couple of buttered bread rolls as she went. Rachel and I simply weren't hungry. I was no sooner out of the door than I went straight back in because something important occurred to me.

"Mum," I said. "OK, I was wrong to say all those nasty things to Mrs Cranston, but did she actually apologize to you for Jenny and Natalie's behaviour to your daughter? I mean, let's face it, if it hadn't been for that I wouldn't have had any need to say anything at all, would I?"

Dad was nodding again and looking at Mum. I could tell he agreed with me. It was then that Mum shocked me to the roots.

"Fen, you and Rachel were exaggerating about the dog game, and well you know it. Jenny has already explained to Mrs Cranston that Natalie went to the loo and left the utility door open by mistake. She also told her that Natalie and she had deliberately brought Rachel back to Jenny's, to get her away from the common where dogs appear every five minutes…"

My mouth was forming an O but I couldn't speak.

"As for the game that Rachel described, she was exaggerating again, I'm afraid. When you have a particular fear like that it can *make* you exaggerate. Mrs Cranston told me Jenny's and Natalie's side of the story, and I'm quite satisfied that they meant no harm. Apparently, they tried to make Digby go inside but he was so excited to be out because he'd been cooped up in the utility room all the time Rachel had been in the house, and all for Rachel's sake, remember. So when they couldn't get him to go back in again, they hung on to his collar and told Rachel to get up in the tree where she was perfectly safe and didn't need to worry. Then they thought they'd throw him two or three balls, before putting him back inside. Unfortunately, that's when you turned up, Fen."

"Don't you see, Mum, it's Natalie again. She's capable of making up anything to protect herself. She's a total liar."

"It was *Jenny* who said all this to her mother, Fen."

"Yes, but I bet you anything, Natalie *made* her say it. Have you asked Rachel if that conversation about Digby happened?"

"No, I haven't, and I don't think there's any point, because Rachel can't recall things properly when she's in her phobic state, but I don't think Jenny would lie to her mother, and I simply can't believe that Natalie could force Jenny into telling lies."

"Oh, Mum, you are *so* wrong. Jenny's completely under Natalie's spell. She'd lie OK."

"Anyway, all I'm saying, Fen, is that if you will go and apologize to Mrs Cranston, I'm prepared to forget the whole thing, but until you do, you can forget all about the café."

My eyes widened incredulously, then narrowed angrily. I breathed in deeply, then exploded.

"Stuff your apology, Mum. I'd rather get bitten by a rattlesnake than apologize to that fat example of human insensitivity. I think you're as bad as she is for not getting to the bottom of things and finding out the real truth." I turned to Dad. "As for you, you're too weak and spineless to stick up for me, even though it's obvious you agree with me, really. You have to go along with the pathetic adult code of practice – all grown-ups stick together."

My dad actually runs on a shorter fuse than me. That's where I get my temper from, so I suppose it was no surprise that he came right back at me.

"I'd be more inclined to see your point of view if you didn't go off at the deep end every five minutes, Fen. It makes you sound totally irrational when you burst out with insults like that. So now you've got *two* people to apologize to. Go away and think about that."

"Don't worry, I'm going!" I yelled, and slammed the kitchen door, before going upstairs two at a time, shutting and locking my bedroom door, and flinging myself down on my bed in floods of angry, hopeless tears.

The worst thing of all – the thing that stuck out like a skyscraper on a green hill – was what Mum said about the café. Well, I've told you I'm single-minded and I'm very determined and nothing was going to make me apologize to Mum. Nothing. Not even the knowledge that I might have to say goodbye to the café job.

That weekend was one of the worst weekends I've ever had in my life. I thought about Luce on Saturday afternoon and wondered how she was getting on. Saturday turned into Sunday and I agonized over whether or not to apologize, but I was still determined not to give in. The only trouble was that time was running out. Monday was the very next day.

It was all supposed to start properly on Monday. My work permit had arrived safely and the whole rota was about to be set in motion. On the very first day it was going to have to be one of the others doing my stint for me.

Then there was Andy. What if her mother decided not to let her continue? No, she wouldn't do that surely? Mr Sorrell was only there for that one weekend wasn't he? Or *was* he?

And what about Jan? Had Mum told her about Andy and me? If so, Jan would be having her doubts about the six of us being suitable. Thank goodness the other four didn't have any problems. I suddenly longed to talk to Tash about everything. I phoned her but there was no reply. Then I remembered she'd said they were going away for the weekend to see some old friends of the family.

I thought about Andy. Did I dare to phone her? What if Mr Sorrell answered? Don't be silly, I told myself, I'm allowed to make a perfectly innocent phone call, aren't I? If he was hovering in the background, I'd just feed the right questions to Andy so she could give me yes/no answers. I tapped in Andy's number.

Chapter 9

"'Allo." It was Dominique answering the French way.

"Hello Dominique, it's Fen here. Could I speak to Andy, please?"

"Yes, of course, my dear, I'll get her. Oh, and Fen, thank you very much for your help on Friday. Meester Sorrell weel understand and accept the café soon, but we have to approach gently. Andy weel explain. Here she ees."

Andy came on the phone. "Hi Fen, thanks for Friday."

"That's OK. You're talking very freely. Isn't your dad around?"

"He's taken Sebastien out to the park. I was just about to phone you, actually."

"Did you make it back to school in time?"

"Yes, I did, thanks to you. Jan was very nice about it, but I'm not sure she'll put up with too many incidents like that."

I sighed and Andy asked if I was OK, so I explained the whole Rachel and the dog episode to her.

"And now Mum says that unless I apologize to Mrs Cranston I can't do the café job," I finished.

"Oh, that's terrible Fen, because I was going to ask you if you could do my turn at the café next Friday, because Dad's actually taking some time off from work and he's not going back to France until the end of next weekend. After that he won't be back for two months, though." Andy's voice softened. "He's not such an ogre as he seems, Fen, he's just overprotective because of being away so much."

"Oh – right," I said, trying to muster some understanding into my voice. Why did I get the impression that Andy was trying to convince herself, not me?

"I think you'd better ask Leah to do next Friday, Andy, and I'm going to ask Tash to do Monday, and we'll all rely on Jan's nice nature, and hope that things will be better the following week."

"Well, I should be OK the following week but what about you? Will your mum relent, do you think?"

It took me less than a second's thought to answer her. "No," I answered, because I knew Mum, and that's where I get my single-mindedness from. "She can be just as stubborn as I can, and neither of us will give in on this."

"What about Jenny's disco? That's next Wednesday, isn't it?"

"Yes. Rachel is just quietly refusing to go and nobody's trying to make her change her mind. The atmosphere in our house is awful. Mum is saying the absolute minimum to me. She's being normal to Rachel, but Rachel seems to have withdrawn right into herself.

Dad is acting strangely. It's as though he's unsure of himself. I think he and Mum have had a big row but they're trying not to let it show.

"Emmy is the only one who's lightening the atmosphere. She keeps making embarrassing jokes like, 'Why is everybody being so noisy in this house?' Then she laughs like a drain because, of course, the house is as silent as a morgue with all these bad feelings floating around."

"Why don't you do something positive like try to get Jenny to crack and admit that Natalie led her on and that they were definitely to blame?"

I was just considering this possibility when I glanced out of the window and spotted a white Renault 5 pulling up outside our house.

"Andy, I've got to go. Guess who's turned up – Jan!"

"Oh, Fen, be careful, won't you? Don't fly off the handle again. Just calmly tell her that everything will be OK because the other four can keep it all going."

I rang off and the phone immediately started ringing again. I picked it up to hear a very raspy faint voice at the other end of the line. It was Leah.

"Fen, I'm really sorry but I've got tonsillitis and there's no way I can do Tuesday. I thought I'd ask Andy if I could swop with her and do Friday... I'm sure to be OK by then."

"Oh…" My heart was sinking and I was beginning to despair of this rota ever working because we were down to three now. "You'll have to swap with Luce, Leah, and do Saturday."

"I can't, because Luce can't manage Tuesday. I've just asked her. What's wrong with Andy?"

"It's a long story. I'll tell you all about it when you're better."

"Oh dear, have I messed up the rota?"

"No, *I've* messed up the rota. Don't worry, Leah, I'll sort something out, you just get well quickly."

"Yeah, thanks Fen."

"Bye."

"Bye."

I could have cried when I put the phone down, but I didn't because I was beyond tears. I went reluctantly downstairs.

"Hello, pet," Aunt Jan greeted me.

Mum obviously hadn't told her the bad news yet.

"Hi," I said, quietly.

Mum pursed her lips and turned her back on me, busying herself with the teapot.

"Oh dear, oh dear, oh dear," said Jan, sizing up the situation immediately. "I smell mother/daughter trouble. Come on, I'll be referee. Let's get it all out in the open. I'm not sitting here in the frost when I'm already freezing cold."

Mum and I looked at each other as if to say, "Who's going to speak first?"

"It's up to Fen to tell you if she's got anything to tell you," Mum said, and I knew in that second that this was my last chance at the café job. It was all so hopeless and I was sick of telling long, involved stories and giving explanations, and having to justify my actions all the time, so in a very flat voice I said that Mum was cross with me because I'd been rude to Mrs Cranston. The reason I'd been rude was because I'd witnessed mental cruelty to my own sister but unfortunately Mrs Cranston was so narrow-minded she only cared about her stupid house getting dirty.

I added in a tired voice with several big sighs that sadly I was stuck with a mother who believed Mrs Cranston's version rather than her own daughter's, and therefore was insisting on an apology to that old witch, and a father who was too weak to tell his wife to get knotted even though he really wanted to...

At that point Mum said, "Right, that does it! You can definitely say goodbye to the café job now. You've just gone a bit too far, young lady."

I ignored her and carried on addressing my words directly to Jan in a monotonous but stinging tone. "Unfortunately, Mum wasn't capable of putting herself in my shoes and imagining that it was her *own* sister – *you*, Jan – clinging to a branch of a tree while two other girls who were supposed to be your friends, chucked balls to a huge German shepherd dog that terrified the life out of you, to make him bound right up to the very tree where you sat trembling. Still – never mind – that's Mum's problem."

"Fen!" Mum shouted.

"Ssh," Jan said, flapping a hand towards Mum and frowning. "I want to hear the rest of this."

In for a penny, in for a pound, I thought wretchedly. "There's no more to tell. Oh, only that Andy didn't have a mother with a migraine on Friday, she had a mother with a big problem. Her problem is Andy's dad. He's never consented to the café job, and he turned up unexpectedly from France. Her mum, who was prepared to let Andy do it as long as the dad wasn't around, took fright like a rabbit in the headlights, the moment he appeared."

Jan's expression, I noticed, was less interested and more irritated now. I decided impulsively to finally kill the Café Club stone dead.

"And Leah's just phoned. She's got tonsillitis and can't do Tuesday."

There was a long silence. I don't know if you've ever heard of a pregnant pause, but I read it in a book the other day, and if it means a silence that seems to go on for nine months, then I reckon the silence in our kitchen was definitely pregnant.

It was Jan who broke it. "I think I preferred sitting in the frost."

"I'm sorry," I said, lamely. "Somebody up there obviously doesn't want me to do this job."

I felt as though I'd had a local anaesthetic and the feeling was coming back and it wasn't too pleasant. Why had I said all those things? Oh, why hadn't I taken Leah's advice and just calmly told Jan everything would be OK because the other four would keep it going?

Jan sighed. "Going back to your own problem, Fen, it's not my place to interfere here really," she began almost hesitantly, "because I've only just heard the gloss on the story, but it sounds to me like the whole thing needs thoroughly investigating before rash judgements and decisions are made."

She was looking at Mum as she said this. Mum looked straight back with that same well-I'm-not-budging expression. Actually it wasn't quite the same. She was taking in what Jan was saying and considering it. I felt the smallest ray of hope. The ray got blacked out with Jan's next words.

"But the fact remains, I have a business to run, and what is happening here is exactly the kind of problem you would associate with thirteen-year-olds, which is why I was so reluctant to take you all on in the first place. Also, I have to say, Luce was not wonderful yesterday. She's a scatterbrain, that girl, and ... I don't know ... trouble seems to follow her around. Apart from that she was wearing ridiculously large, loopy earrings which I had to ask her to remove, so we didn't get off to a particularly good start. In fact, it seems that out of the six of you I can only really rely on Tash and Jaimini at the moment."

She paused and frowned. During that

pause she must have wound herself right up because she suddenly said, "Right, I've made my decision. I've got a neighbour who's been wanting to find a part-time job for ages. If you lot hadn't put your bid in first, I would have offered her a job at the café, but in the light of all this mess, I'm going to offer her that job now."

Mum and I looked at her in horror, then we looked at each other, then back at Jan. Jan stood up abruptly and said, "Take my advice, stop being so stubborn the pair of you, and get this thing sorted." Then she was gone. Until the roar of the Renault's engine fell to a hum and then faded out all together, Mum and I remained like statues.

"Just an apology, that's all it takes," Mum said, softly.

"Never," I told her, even more softly.

The following morning dawned cold and hostile. Rachel had chronic stomach ache and was too ill to go to school. By morning break it was so cold outside that we stayed in a classroom – Jaimini's registration room. Leah wasn't at school because of her tonsillitis, and I had spent the last ten minutes filling the others in on the events of Friday and the long weekend.

The moment when I'd had to confess that Jan had now made other arrangements, was absolutely sickening. I'll never forget the looks on my friends' faces. Andy's expression was one of guilt and pain. She probably felt as responsible as I did for ruining our wonderful scheme. Jaimini looked as though she was desperately trying to appear unconcerned when really I knew she was probably the most upset of any of us, because she never thought she was going to be allowed to do the job in the first place and now it was being taken away from her so soon, through no fault of her own.

Luce was looking openly hacked off – Luce never hid her feelings. Tash just looked very concerned about it all. She immediately put her arm round me. "Don't worry, Fen. For goodness' sake, no one's blaming you, are we?"

Jaimini said, "No, of course not."

Luce shook her head and Andy whispered, "It's my fault as well."

"Nobody's blaming anybody," Tash insisted. "Let's all just try to forget about it and hope that we get a second chance at some point."

"Actually, I wasn't all that great at it anyway," mumbled Luce.

"Oh, I bet you were," Jaimini immediately leapt to her best friend's defence. I suddenly remembered what Jan had said about Luce, but, of course, I wasn't going to say anything.

"It was partly because of that woman you mentioned, Jaimes. You know, the one who accused Louise of pocketing the tip instead of putting it in the box."

"Yes, I can't forget her in a hurry," Jaimini said with feeling.

Again I didn't say anything but I was as curious as the others to know what had happened this time. Tash was wrinkling her forehead, deep in concentration.

"What was the name on her badge again, Jaimini?"

"Um… Maggie I think… Yes, Maggie."

Tash was obviously plumbing the depths of her memory judging from the intense expression on her face.

"Go on, Luce, what happened?" I urged her.

"Well, as soon as the woman appeared, Louise said to Jan, 'I don't care what table she sits at, *I'm* not serving her. She's really got it in for me.'

"Jan told Louise not to worry and said she'd serve the woman herself. She also stressed that *I* mustn't serve, unless specifically asked by Jan. Well, the first thing the woman – Maggie – did was to deliberately leave her bag sticking out, and typically it was Louise who tripped over it. Louise looked daggers but managed to mumble an apology and the woman said something like, 'Downright clumsiness.' Then…" Here Luce paused and her eyes went all gooey, "…who should walk in but Mr Dreamy."

"Mr Dreamy???" the rest of us said in bewildered chorus.

"You know – Billabong."

"Billabong!" we exclaimed, inching forward a little because Luce's story was really livening up. Luce herself looked rapt.

"I really thought my luck was in. I went straight over to him with my little pad and said, 'Hello Mr Blundell, and what may I get you today?'

"He got quite a shock when he realized it was me, I can tell you. He looked totally embarrassed but I was sure he was pleased to see me. Anyway before I had even put pen to paper Jan suddenly appeared and said, 'Thank you, Lucy, I'll deal with this. Kevin needs you for some washing-up.'

"Bad luck, Lucy," called out Mr Dreamy.

"I could see that Jan wasn't too happy and I was right. 'I thought I told you not to serve – by which I also mean take orders – unless I specifically ask,' she snapped at me a minute later over the washing-up. I apologized and said that I had thought she was referring to Maggie only when she said that. She said, 'Don't let it happen again.'

"I did the washing-up as fast as I could so I

could get back to Mr Dreamy. When I went back into the café – SHOCK HORROR! – this amazing-looking woman was sitting right next to him and they were looking into each other's eyes, you know."

"Yes, we know," said Tash, who was impatient for the story to move on. We all were.

"Well, I wanted to get a better look at her, so I went to clear the table next to theirs. I cleared it as slowly as I could so I had plenty of time to notice every detail, like the fact that their hands touched three times, their eyes met nearly all the time, her hair – long chestnut curls – fell on his shoulder twice. They laughed at the tiniest thing and under the table their feet were touching."

"How did you manage to see under the table?" Jaimini asked.

"I deliberately dropped a spoon, then took my time bending down to pick it up."

"Yes, OK go on," Tash said.

"What happened next was the awful bit. I was walking towards the kitchen with a loaded tray because I didn't dare spend any more time clearing that table, when Jan grabbed the tray from me and said, 'For goodness' sake, concentrate Luce, you've just cleared the table I laid three minutes ago. I've been trying to attract your attention for ages but you were so busy staring at the customers that you didn't notice me. Rule number one: keep your wits about you the whole time. You must always be aware of everything that's going on around you in a café. Remember that.'

"I apologized for the second time, and no sooner had Jan marched off with the tray than Louise sidled past me and whispered, 'For pity's sake take that woman at number six an iced soda. She's been waiting for ages.' It's anybody's guess why she wanted iced soda in this freezing cold weather, but she did.

"Of course it was Maggie at table six so I didn't know what to do, because Jan had made it quite clear that I wasn't to serve again and yet she'd also agreed that she would deal with the lady so that Louise didn't have to. I was just heading off to get Jan to ask her what to do, when Louise yanked me back and squealed, 'What are you doing, Lucy? Jan'll go spare if you interrupt her when she's taking an order.' Jan was actually taking an order at a table for six people and it sounded long and involved. I could tell she wouldn't be finished for quite a few minutes and we couldn't leave Maggie that long when she'd already been waiting for ages."

"So what did you do?" I asked, impatient like the others to know how this tale was going to turn out.

"I told Louise that I wasn't allowed to serve anyone, and Louise said, 'Yes but in this instance you'll just have to. It's only an iced soda, after all.'

"'Jan's told me twice not to serve,' I hissed at Louise.

"'But Jan also said that I didn't have to deal with that awful woman at all, and Mark's busy on the phone, so that only leaves you. Go on, Luce. Hurry up.'

"Without our realizing it, our voices had apparently been getting louder and louder and Jan was giving us meaningful looks, trying to get us to shut up, but Louise and I were both oblivious to all this because neither of us wanted to deal with the awful Maggie.

"'But why can't you?' I asked Louise, raising my voice.

"'Let's just say that it's a personality clash,' Louise answered, also raising her voice.

"At that point Maggie stood up noisily and called over to Jan, 'Manageress, I'm sorry to interrupt you, but I really must complain about this waitress refusing to serve me.' Jan calmly said, 'Excuse me for two seconds, please,' to the people at the table where she was taking the order. I tried my best to look innocent and unconcerned because I could feel Billabong's eyes boring into me, and I didn't want him to see me in a bad light.

"Maggie carried on ranting at Jan. 'I have just heard with my very own ears, this girl... (she flung an accusing finger at Louise when she said that) ...refusing to serve me because of what she describes as a personality clash!' Maggie cast her eyes round the café as if to whip up a bit of support for her argument."

'That's just what she did when I was on duty," Jaimini said.

"She sounds like a real troublemaker," said Andy.

"It sounds worse than that to me," Tash commented thoughtfully. "She's obviously deliberately targeting Louise. I wish I could remember where I've seen that name on that badge before," she added.

"What happened next?" I asked Luce.

"Maggie went on to address Louise. 'That's three times I've been subjected to your rudeness, miss.'

"That must have made something snap in Louise, because she turned her wrath on Maggie and said with great sarcasm, 'Well, you needn't worry, madam, because this is my last day working here so we won't have to put up with each other ever again.'

"'Well, in that case,' Maggie retorted, 'I pity your new employer, because one simply can't afford to have personality clashes, particularly if there are clients involved.'

"Jan intervened hastily before things got

any worse. She softly apologized to Maggie for everything, urged her to sit down, got her the iced soda herself, and told her that, of course, there would be no question of her having to pay the bill on this occasion. Jan then glided over to the other table and apologized to the customers she had kept waiting, who were really understanding and pleasant.

"Louise and I worked under a cloud, with Mark, who was totally oblivious of all this, for another hour before the place shut. Mr Dreamy and his partner had disappeared during the Maggie episode, without my even noticing.

"As soon as the CLOSED sign was in place, Jan gave both Louise and me a piece of her mind. She gave me another telling off for not concentrating, and for standing about discussing clients, then she really laid into Louise. 'You are much more experienced than Lucy,' she said, 'and should know better. I don't care if it *is* your last day, you had no right to be rude to that lady, however unfair she was towards you. I'm seriously thinking that she had a point, actually. Perhaps I ought to make it quite clear to the manageress of ClairHair that your customer relations aren't all they should be. She did phone for a reference and I gave you a very glowing one at the time, but I have to say, I was not impressed by your behaviour today, and I hate to think what damage it's done to my own trade.'

"Louise and I hung our heads in shame. I felt really sorry for Louise. Jan seemed to be overreacting rather..."

"That's *it*!" Tash suddenly interjected, excitedly. "Maggie! I know where I've seen that name on a badge – at ClairHair. That was the hairdresser who was sweeping the floor when we were talking to Lyn about Louise. Don't you remember, Fen, Lyn said, 'I think Glenda's already got someone to fill my job when I leave,' and the one who was sweeping, called Maggie, said, 'Yes, she has,' in a really unpleasant tone of voice."

"You're right, Tash," I said. "It's been

bugging me where I'd seen that face before, but now I come to think of it, I hardly glanced at her at ClairHair, but it was her voice I recognized at the café."

"You don't think Jan would really spoil Louise's chances at ClairHair by telling Glenda what happened, do you?" Luce asked, sounding worried.

"That's it!" Tash cried for the second time. "Maggie set this whole thing up to try to prevent Louise from working at ClairHair."

"But why?" asked Andy.

"Because," Tash explained, "she wants the job herself."

"But she's got a job," Jaimini pointed out.

"Yes, but not as a stylist," Tash went on. "That's why she sounded so hacked off, because Glenda had decided to bring in an outsider instead of promoting her."

"Oh dear, what if Jan *does* decide to phone Glenda?" Luce said, anxiously.

"Or worse still, what if she's already phoned? I feel so responsible. It'll be my fault if Louise loses out on her new job."

"Let's go to ClairHair, Tash, and explain everything to Glenda. It's the least we can do for Louise," I said impulsively, grabbing Tash by the arm.

"What? Now?" screeched Tash. "We can't just walk out of school?"

"Yes, we can," I told her, firmly.

Chapter 10

"Go on!" Andy immediately said, and Jaimini and Luce were quick to try and persuade us, too.

"Even if Jan doesn't phone Glenda," Jaimini pointed out, "Maggie is sure to make Louise's life hell at ClairHair."

"Yes," Luce agreed. "Poor Louise, walking into her lovely new job to find that nasty baggage there."

We looked at each other and realization dawned on us all at exactly the same moment. Maggie was obviously hoping that Louise would do exactly that. She'd walk into her nice, new place of work, take one look at who she had to work with, and walk straight out again. After all, who could bear to work with someone who hated your guts and had already accused you of bad customer relations?

"Come on," I urged Tash, "we need to get down there and make sure Glenda gets the true version of the facts before it's too late."

"You go with Fen, Luce," Tash suggested, sensibly. "After all, you're the one who witnessed the trouble at the café."

Luce looked unsure but nodded. "Yeah, OK. Let's get going while it's still break. We'll be back by lunchtime. Hopefully, no one will miss us by then."

So Luce and I surreptitiously slipped off the school premises and half walked, half ran all the way to ClairHair. We didn't really have any firm idea of what we were going to say when we got there, but we both felt very strongly about our mission, so I suppose we just thought our words would flow spontaneously when we walked in.

What I had forgotten was that there would, of course, be customers in the hairdresser's. I had imagined it was going to be empty, purely because I was picturing it as it had been the last time Tash and I were there. So naturally it came as quite a shock to walk into a bustling atmosphere with hairdriers buzzing, shower taps spraying and little pockets of happy conversation going on all over the place.

I spotted Glenda straight away, teetering across the room on her high heels, carrying a plastic container and a little tiny brush. Her eyelashes were flapping away but she didn't look her usual jaunty self. In fact, she looked decidedly stressed.

"There's Maggie, over there," Luce whispered to me, sounding as nervous as I felt. Maggie was smiling into a mirror as she cut the hair of a pretty woman who looked about thirty-five. I met the woman's eyes through the mirror but Maggie hadn't yet noticed us. Luce and I quickly scanned the rest of the salon. There was no sign of Louise, unless she was out at the back.

I noticed two other hairdressers. One of them was the girl who had also been sweeping the floor last time we were in the salon. The other was a girl of about seventeen who was washing someone's hair. I'd never seen her before. She very deftly whipped her customer's hair into a neat turban, draped a fresh towel round her shoulders, guided her over to a mirror and approached us with a welcoming smile on her face.

"Hello," she said warmly. "Did you want to make an appointment?"

"No, not exactly," stumbled Luce. The girl was eyeing Luce's thick mass of hair and probably wondering where one would start with such a mop. I came to the rescue.

"We wondered if we could possibly have a quick word with Glenda?"

"Yes, of course," the girl said. The name on her badge said Sally. "Who shall I say it is?" she asked me.

"Um … she won't know my name," I said, feeling foolish.

Sally didn't seem to find anything unusual in our behaviour, which gave a little boost to my confidence. Maggie still hadn't noticed us and we sidled round to the very end of the reception desk where we were just out of view.

Glenda had a strained look on her face as she came up to the desk. She saw me, looked puzzled for a second as if she was trying to place me, then smiled in recognition. "Hello dear, what can I do for you?"

"I'm terribly sorry to disturb you," I began politely, "because I can see you're really busy. It's about Louise Shrimpton."

"Don't talk to me about Louise Shrimpton. She's the reason why I'm so busy."

Luce and I must have looked puzzled because she went on, "Louise had hardly stepped through the door when she suddenly announced that the whole thing had been one huge mistake, and that for personal reasons she couldn't take the job after all. I was not best pleased, I can tell you."

Glenda tutted away, her eyelashes batting in sympathetic annoyance and even her bees'-nest hair nodding in agreement. Luce and I exchanged disappointed looks. The damage had probably been done, but there was still a small chance that we could avert it.

"The thing is, Glenda, we came to try and defend Louise."

Luce chipped in at that point, "You see, I was working in the café on Saturday, and that woman over there – Maggie – came in. To cut a long story short she got Louise into trouble for doing absolutely nothing wrong."

Glenda had lowered her head as if she was looking over the top of bifocals, even though she wasn't wearing glasses. I took over from Luce, speaking softly to be sure Maggie wouldn't hear me.

"That was the third time Maggie had been in the café, and all three times she got Louise into trouble and made a big public scene about it. We're certain she did it on purpose so that Louise wouldn't want to work here, when she realized who she'd have to work with. You see, each time Maggie caused a scene at the café, one of our group of friends witnessed it, and thought she was way out of order. At first we wondered if she was trying to get my aunt Jan, the manageress of the café, to give Louise a bad reference."

"Well, well, well," said Glenda. It was impossible to know how she was digesting our information. Her gaze didn't alter but her eyes narrowed. She was thinking hard. Eventually she spoke, softly and gravely.

"Thank you very much for taking the trouble to come, girls. It says a great deal about your character that you came specially to explain all that. I just want you to know that if Louise Shrimpton is not here in her new job as a stylist by lunchtime, and if Maggie Swan is not out for good, my name is not Glenda Clair!"

So that's where the name ClairHair came from, I thought, as Glenda carried on talking.

"That Maggie has been angling after a job as a stylist for a long time now, but for various reasons she isn't cut out to be one, if you'll excuse the pun! What you've just told me is the last straw as far as I'm concerned. It also says a great deal about Louise, that she didn't start moaning about Maggie. She simply left the salon, sacrificing her job *and* my good opinion of her, in the process."

Luce and I couldn't help our eyes straying over to where Maggie was chatting and clipping brightly. Glenda caught our glance.

"I'm not going to risk a scene while she's cutting someone's hair," she explained in a loud whisper. "Look, I suggest you two go now because I don't want her to see you here. It's better that she doesn't know who dobbed on her."

"Yes, right," we agreed hastily, shuffling towards the door and smiling at the word "dobbed" coming from an adult. We sneaked out, but not before Glenda had given us a broad wink. Her false eyelashes were navy blue and even though I was very fond of her, I thought her eyelashes were gross. Luce obviously didn't agree.

"By the way, your eyelashes are wonderful!" she complimented Glenda.

"I'll let you into a secret, my dears," Glenda whispered confidentially, "...they're false."

Well, as you can imagine, we had no sooner

shut the salon door behind us, than we fell about in gales of laughter in front of various surprised shoppers. Glenda was such a character. Fancy thinking we hadn't realized her eyelashes were false!

"Mission accomplished and back to school?" I said brightly to Luce.

"While we're here, let's just nip into the High Street. I keep forgetting to bring my money for those pull-through earrings, but I've remembered it today, and I'm certain they'll be gone if I leave it till after school. In fact, I'm praying they haven't gone already."

"Oh, Luce, don't you think we ought to get back? I don't want to get into any more trouble than I'm already in."

"It won't take five minutes, Fen. Oh, *please*, go on – five minutes won't make any difference.

"Come on, then. Let's run."

The jeweller's was right next door to the café, so we stopped running when we got nearer. I didn't want Jan to see me through the window and report to Mum that on top of all my other crimes, I'd also been skiving school.

"Look, Fen," Luce suddenly said, stopping abruptly. "That's your sister's friend, isn't it? What's her name – Jenny?"

Luce was right. It was a very worried, furtive-looking Jenny.

"Whatever is she doing?" Luce asked me softly.

We slipped into a shop entrance and peered out surreptitiously to watch Jenny without her seeing us. She seemed to be keeping guard. She was right outside the jeweller's looking up and down the High Street.

"Keep back," I warned Luce, "I don't want her to see us."

"Why not?" Luce demanded. "For goodness' sake, Fen, she's not a teacher or anything. And anyway *she* must be skiving too."

"I can't explain. It's a long story, Luce, but unless I'm very much mistaken, there's a long-legged, blonde-haired American girl in the café, also aged nine… I'm going to talk to Jenny."

Luce shook her head as though I was totally mad. "Whatever you say, Fen. I'll go into the jeweller's, OK?"

Jenny gasped as she saw me approach, then she immediately turned towards the café.

"What's up, Jenny?" I asked as I got up to her and Luce went into the jeweller's. "Come on, I can see you're scared... It's Natalie, isn't it?"

At first she said, "No, course not," then she crumbled. She'd obviously had enough. She nodded dumbly and tears came into her eyes. Poor kid. It was all falling into place now. Jenny was being manipulated by Natalie.

"I'm sorry about the dog, Fen... She made me. I had no choice because..."

"Never mind that, Jenny. I know it's not your fault, it's OK, but whatever are you doing here?"

"Natalie's stolen money from my mum's purse. She's eating beefburgers and chips in the café and I've got to keep watch and tell her if I see anyone we know. She made me skive off school..."

"But *how* did she make you? Whatever evil method does she use?"

Jenny's eyes filled up again and I didn't want her to be any more upset so I told her not to bother explaining just now.

"Don't worry," I said, patting her shoulder. "I'll get you out of this. I'm not sure how, but I will."

Luce was just coming out of the jeweller's. She gave me the thumbs up and patted her pocket. I suddenly felt decisive. "Follow me."

"What's going on, Fen?" Luce asked.

"That American girl I told you about – the one who's responsible for ruining our café work – she's in there. Come on," I said, setting my lips determinedly. I turned round. Jenny was still rooted to the spot. I took her hand and more or less dragged her round the back of the café.

"Natalie'll kill me, Fen."

"No, she won't."

We went into the kitchen through the back door. Kevin was deftly juggling three frying pans and two other pans. There was steam everywhere.

"Wrong door, ladies," he said, hardly glancing up, "unless you want a Turkish bath, that is."

"Where's Jan?" I asked, not feeling in the mood for Kevin's wit. My question was answered by Jan herself.

"Whatever are you doing here, Fen?" came her surprised-sounding voice as she stopped in her tracks just inside the kitchen door.

"I can't explain but it's really important. There's a girl in the café with a blonde ponytail…"

"Yes, I've been wondering about her. She should be at school. I questioned her and she said she was on holiday over here and her mum would be joining her shortly. I didn't believe her because that accent of hers sounds totally phoney."

What! Don't say she's pulled the wool over our eyes totally, I thought. I didn't have time to dwell on it. Jenny told us Natalie's phone number and Jan went to phone her mother. I couldn't hear what Jan was saying because the phone was in the passage near the toilets, and I didn't want to risk Natalie seeing me if she decided to go to the loo, or the Jim, as she called it. "The Jim!" How stupid it sounded. Surely Natalie knew it was the "john" not the "Jim". Or did she?

"Well," said Jan, coming back into the kitchen, "Natalie's mother is about as American as I am, and she had no idea at all that her daughter wasn't at school. She sounded pretty upset. She'll be here in a few minutes."

Jan paused and eyed me thoughtfully. "Is this the one you were telling me about, Fen?"

I nodded. Jan's lips tightened.

"What if Natalie finishes her burger and goes out and sees that I'm not there, before her mum gets here?" asked Jenny, in a small voice.

"Hm," said Jan and she slipped into the café, returning a moment later to say, "Don't worry, she's not quite finished, and she's ordered ice-cream for afters." Jan turned to

Jenny. "What about you, pet? What have you had to eat?"

"Nothing," Jenny whispered, "but I'm not hungry," she added.

Debra and Becky came through to the kitchen looking hot and tired and rather taken aback to see us three standing there.

"Day off school?" asked Becky.

"No … it's complicated," I answered.

"Oh, life is sooooo complicated," sang Kevin, in a loud tuneless voice. We all laughed but he carried on singing, oblivious to all around him. I noticed two trickles of sweat, one on either side of his face. He dumped a couple of frying pans in the washing-up and called out, "Service, someone … and make it snappy!" Becky and Debra were back in the café, so I washed the pans myself.

"Excellent work! Take ten merits and a star," Kevin said to me in a posh voice. We were all laughing as Jan came back in and said, "Natalie's mother is here – and so is your mother, Fen, with Rachel. I suggest we go through and join them."

So we trooped in, silent and wide-eyed. My heart was banging my rib cage. The web was closing in on Natalie. Surely she wouldn't be able to get out of this mess. I felt a second's pity for her, but it dissolved rapidly as a picture of Rachel in the tree flashed into my head.

I'll never forget the look on Natalie's face as she looked up from absorbedly smearing her beefburger with a thick coating of tomato sauce, to see us all standing there in a semi-circle around her table. Her fork stopped half-way to her mouth, and her eyes went rapidly through a series of expressions that told the story of her thoughts in about three seconds. They went from neutral to alarm to defiance to panic, and finally settled on stubbornness.

She calmly put the fork into her mouth and very slowly chewed the beefburger. You had to hand it to her, her front was amazing. That stubbornness, though, only served to fuel the fire of our fury. It was her mother who spoke first, trying not to raise her voice, trying not to sound too angry in public. Her accent was definitely English; I think from somewhere in the Midlands.

"What are you doing here, young lady?"

No answer.

"If you had any idea of the trouble you've caused, young lady…"

No answer. Natalie even had the cheek to carry on eating. Jan and Mum rolled their eyes at each other. Mum moved closer to me and put an arm round my shoulder. Still nobody spoke but Natalie's mother. Don't ask me if there was anybody else in the café. At that moment my attention was totally on the scene before my eyes.

"The game's up, my girl, and it's time for you to do a lot of thinking, apologizing and changing. I had a long talk with Mrs Cranston this afternoon."

Silence.

"You can forget all about your disco tomorrow night, you know…"

Still silence, but the stubborn look was definitely gone. She was cracking.

"I thought you said she was American," Luce said to me, in a loud aside. Natalie's mother picked it up.

"American!" she squawked. "Not another whopper, young lady! I've been talking to Jenny's mum, and when she mentioned someone called Natalie, I says, 'Natalie? Who's she when she's at home?' And Jenny's mum says, 'It's your daughter,' and I says, 'Well, I can assure you, Mrs Cranston, the only daughter I've got's called Noreen.'"

Noreen! So Jan was right! And at this moment, Noreen was beginning to look very uncomfortable.

Mum obviously thought it was time to break up the party. "Come on, let's get back home," she said to Rachel and me.

"Can I go to school for the afternoon?" Rachel asked Mum, surprising us all. "We're doing portrait painting in pairs, you see," she explained. "Come on, Jenny, let's paint each other's portraits."

And that's when Natalie cracked.

"You said you'd *never* be her partner," she

suddenly wailed at Jenny, in a pathetic voice with not a trace of American accent.

"I'm Rachel's partner," Jenny answered firmly. "We're always partners, aren't we, Rachel?"

Rachel nodded and linked her arm through Jenny's. "Yeah, course," she said. They stood there together, not defiantly but solidly, and it was just too much for poor weak Noreen from the Midlands to cope with. Her face dissolved from a silly scowl to a crumply, tearful mess, yet no one seemed to be able to summon up any sympathy. It was Jan who took control.

"I think you need to get Noreen home, Mrs...?"

"Mrs Shore."

"Let me help you," Jan went on, and she helped the snuffly Noreen to her feet and ushered both her and her shell-shocked mother gently out of the café.

"I'm sorry about all this," Mrs Shore kept saying.

"Don't worry," Jan reassured her, then they were gone.

I looked round. Fortunately the only people in the café were eight ladies who were dressed as though they'd just been to an aerobics class or something. They were chatting and laughing so loudly that they must have been oblivious to our little drama.

"Smart move, Fen," said Jan, patting my back.

"What?" I asked.

"Getting me to phone her mum like that. Smart move." Then she set to, briskly clearing Noreen's table.

Fancy Natalie turning out to be Noreen. Life was weird.

"How did you know I'd be here anyway?" I asked Mum.

"Jan phoned me after she'd phoned Natalie's – I mean Noreen's – mum."

"Why?" I asked, still puzzled.

"Well, Jan was worried when you suddenly appeared at the café when you should have been at school. But I wanted to talk to you, anyway. I was going to come and collect you early from school."

"From school?" I squeaked, wondering what on earth Mum wanted to say that could be so important that she was going to interrupt my day at school.

"It was because of something Rachel said," Mum began to explain. "Tell Fen what you told me this morning, Rachel."

Rachel looked down and I didn't catch what she said the first time. She repeated it more loudly.

"It was Natalie who cut the dress."

I gasped and felt instant anger welling up inside me. I knew immediately what had happened, and Rachel's explanation proved me right.

"She made me say it was you, Fen. First she told me to say it was Emmy, but I told her no one would believe that because Emmy would never be able to manage pinking shears. Then she said I had to blame it on you and make absolutely sure Mum and Dad didn't suspect anything. She said that if anyone ever found out that it was she who did it, she'd arrange for something awful to happen to me. She didn't say what, she just said 'something awful'."

A couple of big tears slid down Rachel's pale cheeks.

"I thought she might harm one of my family," she gulped.

At that moment I hated Natalie or Noreen or whoever she was, even more than before, if that was possible. I reached for Rachel's hand and gave it a squeeze.

"I had to use the pinking shears this morning," Mum carried on, "and while I was using them I kept thinking there was something odd about them but I couldn't work out what it was. Then it hit me in a flash. I went straight up to Rachel's room and brought her cut dress down. I was right. The indents of the serrated edge on the dress were larger than the ones my pinking shears made. Rachel's dress had not been cut with our pinking shears at all. So I confronted Rachel and she confessed everything.

"But *why* did Natalie" (it's no good, I'll never get used to Noreen) "cut your best dress in the first place, Rachel?"

"Because I took it to school to show Jenny what I was going to wear for her disco, and she asked if she could take it home to show her mum. When she came to school the next day, she said she'd given the dress to Natalie because Natalie wanted to try it on. Anyway, Natalie came to our school playground again, and gave me back the dress – all cut… She pretended she did it to make it look nicer, but I know she didn't. She did it because she didn't want me at Jenny's disco. When I said that, she told me that she'd got special powers and she could make things happen – really bad things…"

Jenny carried on.

"She told *me* that if I wouldn't be her best friend, she'd get her dad to take away our house and all our money and even Digby, because she said her dad's a very important person in politics, even more important than the Prime Minister. But he works in secret and that's why there are never any pictures of him on the telly or anything."

Mum nodded understandingly at Jenny,

then turned back to me.

"As soon as I realized what Natalie was actually capable of, I knew I'd misjudged you over the dog episode, Fen. I went straight round to Mrs Cranston's and we had a long chat. I owe you a big apology, Fen," Mum said. "I really am sorry, love, I got it completely wrong. And your father, as usual, was right. He's going to be very smug about that, I expect."

Mum laughed. It was nice to feel happiness beginning to filter into our lives again. Mum's next words let loose another little spurt of happiness.

"I think Jan's looking forward to your first stint at four o'clock today."

"Wow!" I cried, which brought Jan over.

"The name's Jan, not wow!" she joked, "and you're all reinstated. Leah phoned me to say she's much better. It was just a bad throat, not tonsillitis after all, so she'll be able to work tomorrow. That just leaves Andy to sort out, and as that's likely to be a limited problem, I'm prepared to put up with it."

I couldn't help it, I gave Jan a great big hug and a smacking kiss. The aerobics ladies looked at us as though we were completely nuts.

Mum took first Rachel and Jenny, and then me and Luce, back to school. She had a quick word of explanation with our school secretary, then took me to one side before she went.

"Apparently, Noreen's mother and father are in the process of separating, and that, combined with the upheaval of the move to a new place, have really affected Noreen's emotions. I know it's unthinkable at the moment, but once we're back to a little more normality, I'd like you *and* Rachel to think sympathetically about Noreen. She needs support and help and we can all do our bit."

Mum was sensible and wise, but she was right, at the moment it was unthinkable.

The afternoon was another educational blank for me. My mind was going over and over the events of the morning, and also looking ahead excitedly but nervously to four o'clock.

It was wonderful, my first Monday at proper work. Between them, Jan, Mark and Kevin managed to keep me more or less chained to the kitchen sink. Even so, I felt like a real member of the working world. I couldn't believe it when Jan came into the kitchen and said I could stop work and get ready to go.

I looked at the clock when she'd gone back into the café, and saw that it was only ten to six. Jan's watch must be fast, I thought, so I went into the café after her, dripping soapy washing-up water as I went.

In the café I stood stock still and stared. I couldn't believe the transformation that had happened. There were balloons hanging everywhere in great bright clusters. Line after line of paper chains scooped and dangled above my head. The two largest tables had been put together and occupied the central space in the café. A bright pink and purple tasselled tablecloth draped down to the floor on all sides. Crackers and hats, sausage rolls and chocolate crunch, pizza and creamy sponge cake, covered the table.

As I stared, a series of loud pops erupted, and a mass of frothy coloured fronds shot up high and trickled down all over the place. A wave of laughter engulfed me. You can guess who was there sitting round that table, can't you? Tash, Jaimini, Luce, Andy, Leah, Rachel, Emmy, Mum, Dad and Jan – all grinning from ear to ear at the surprise they'd made for me – and all there to share with me the wonderful launch of the Café Club.

I wiped my hands on the apron and sat down between Tash and Jan. Jan slipped something into my hand under the table. It was a little brown envelope, my first pay packet. My eyes met hers and we both burst into giggles. Don't ask me why. I haven't a clue, but it's a moment that will stick in my mind for ever.

Join

Would you and your friends like to know more about Fen, Tash, Leah, Andy, Jaimini and Luce?

We have produced a special bookmark to commemorate the launch of the Café Club series. To get yours free, together with a special newsletter about Fen and her friends, their creator, author Ann Bryant, and advance information about what's coming next in the series, write (enclosing a self-addressed label, please) to:

The Café Club
c/o the Publicity Department
Scholastic Children's Books
Commonwealth House
1-19 New Oxford Street
London WC1A 1NU

We look forward to hearing from you!

Make room for the next helping of...

2: LEAH DISCOVERS BOYS

The conversation wasn't easy on the way to Fen's house. Danny walked between us. It was nice to feel protected in the dark. We stuck to safe subjects like teachers at school. Danny said that he liked Mrs Merle too, and I thought how nice it was that we were already finding things we had in common.

We said goodbye to Fen at her house and I suddenly felt nervous to be on my own with Danny. I also felt excited. I wondered if he was going to be my first boyfriend. Danny was talking about his computer. He was crazy on computers. I wasn't interested in the slightest but I liked listening to the sound of his voice and it gave me the chance to daydream.

I was imagining going to the cinema with him. I knew I'd be the envy of a lot of other girls because he was good-looking and tall, and a very good runner. He'd even run for the county. I imagined myself amongst the on-lookers at an athletics meeting, watching Danny sprinting towards the finishing tape... Yes! He's *won*!

The crowd burst into cheers as they clapped their hands sore, but Danny only had eyes for me as he fought his way through eager autograph hunters to be at my side. His eyes never left my face as he got nearer and nearer and...

"We're here, aren't we?" his voice came crashing into my imaginings.

"Yes ... we are..." I said, blushing furiously and thinking thank goodness it's dark, and thank triple goodness he can't mind-read.

by R.L. Stine

Reader beware, you're in for a scare!

These terrifying tales will send shivers up your spine . . .

Available now:

Look out for:

*If you like animals, then you'll love
Hippo Animal Stories!*

Look out for:

Animal Rescue by **Bette Paul**

Tessa finds life in the country *so* different from life in
the town. Will she ever be accepted? But everything
changes when she meets Nora and Ned who run the
village animal sanctuary, and becomes involved in a
struggle to save the badgers of Delves Wood
from destruction . . .

Thunderfoot by **Deborah van der Beek**

Mel Whitby has always loved horses, and when she
comes across an enormous by neglected horse in a
railway field, she desperately wants to take care of it.
But little does she know that taking care of
Thunderfoot will change her life forever . . .

A Foxcub Named Freedom
by **Brenda Jobling**

A vixen lies seriously injured in the undergrowth. Her
young son comes to her for comfort and warmth. The
cub wants to help his mother to safety, but it is
impossible. The vixen, sensing danger, nudges him
away, caring nothing for herself – only for
his freedom . . .

Hippo Fantasy

Lose yourself in a whole new world, a world where anything is possible – from wizards and dragons, to time travel and new civilizations . . . Gripping, thrilling, scary and funny by turns, these Hippo Fantasy titles will hold you captivated to the very last page.

The Night of Wishes
Michael Ende (author of *The Neverending Story*)

Malcolm and the Cloud-Stealer
Douglas Hill

The Wednesday Wizard
Sherryl Jordan

Ratspell
Paddy Mounter

Rowan of Rin
Emily Rodda

The Practical Princess
Jay Williams